KIDS' STUFF

LEFT BANK
Collection Number 6

Blue Heron Publishing, Inc.
Hillsboro, Oregon

Editor: Linny Stovall

Associate Editors: Stephen J. Beard, David Sorsoli

Publisher: Dennis Stovall

Copy Editor: Sandra Dorr

Advertising: Linny Stovall

Interior Design: Dennis Stovall

Interior Art: Miles Inada

Cover Art: Cyan Sechel

Cover Design: Marcia Barrentine

Advisors: Ann Chandonnet, Madeline DeFrees, David James Duncan, Katherine Dunn, Jim Hepworth, Ursula K. Le Guin, Lynda Sexson, J. T. Stewart, Alan Twigg, Lyle Weis, Shawn Wong.

Editorial correspondence: Linny Stovall or Stephen Beard, Left Bank, Blue Heron Publishing, Inc., 24450 N.W. Hansen Road, Hillsboro, Oregon 97124. Submissions are welcome if accompanied by a self-addressed, stamped envelope. Otherwise, they will not be returned. Prefer authors who have a strong connection to the Pacific Northwest. Submissions are read during a period beginning one month before the deadline (see current guidelines) and ending one month after. Editorial guidelines are available on request (include SASE).

Left Bank is a series of thematic collections published semiannually by Blue Heron Publishing, Inc., 24450 N.W. Hansen Road, Hillsboro, Oregon 97124. Single editions/collections are US$9.95 (plus $2 s&h). Subscriptions (two editions/collections) are available for $16. Left Bank is distributed to the book trade and libraries in the United States by Consortium Book Sales and Distribution, 1045 Westgate Drive, Saint Paul, Minnesota 55114-1065; and in Canada by Orca Book Publishers, Ltd., Box 5626, Station B, Victoria, B.C. V8V 3W1.

Palestine © 1993 Joe Sacco/Fantagraphics. Reprinted with permission, not in its original form. Poem excerpt from the limited-edition chapbook, The Kingdom at Hand, © 1993 by David Axelrod. Reprinted by permission of Ice River Press. Excerpt adapted from The Way We Never Were, copyright © 1992 by BasicBooks, a division of HarperCollins Publishers, Inc. Reprinted with permission of BasicBooks, a division of HarperCollins, Inc.

Left Bank #6: Kids' Stuff

First edition, June 1994

Copyright © 1994 by Blue Heron Publishing, Inc.

ISBN 0-936085-26-6
ISSN 1056-7429

Contents

FOREWORD 5
TONGUE TIED 7
    Brian Doyle
LIFE WITH FATHER 9
    Mikal Gilmore
WHY GOOD KIDS GROW UP BAD 18
    Ann Rule
THE KINGDOM AT HAND (EXCERPT 1) 27
    David Axelrod
THE DELIVERATOR 30
    Neal Stephenson
PHOTOGRAPHS 45
    Marly Stone
THE HAPPIEST PLACE ON EARTH 49
    Sallie Tisdale
THE ROOT OF THE GAME 61
    Juan Armando Epple
    Translated by Ken Inness
LA RAIZ DEL JUEGO 65
    Juan Armando Epple
A WING AND A PRAYER 69
    Virginia Euwer Wolff

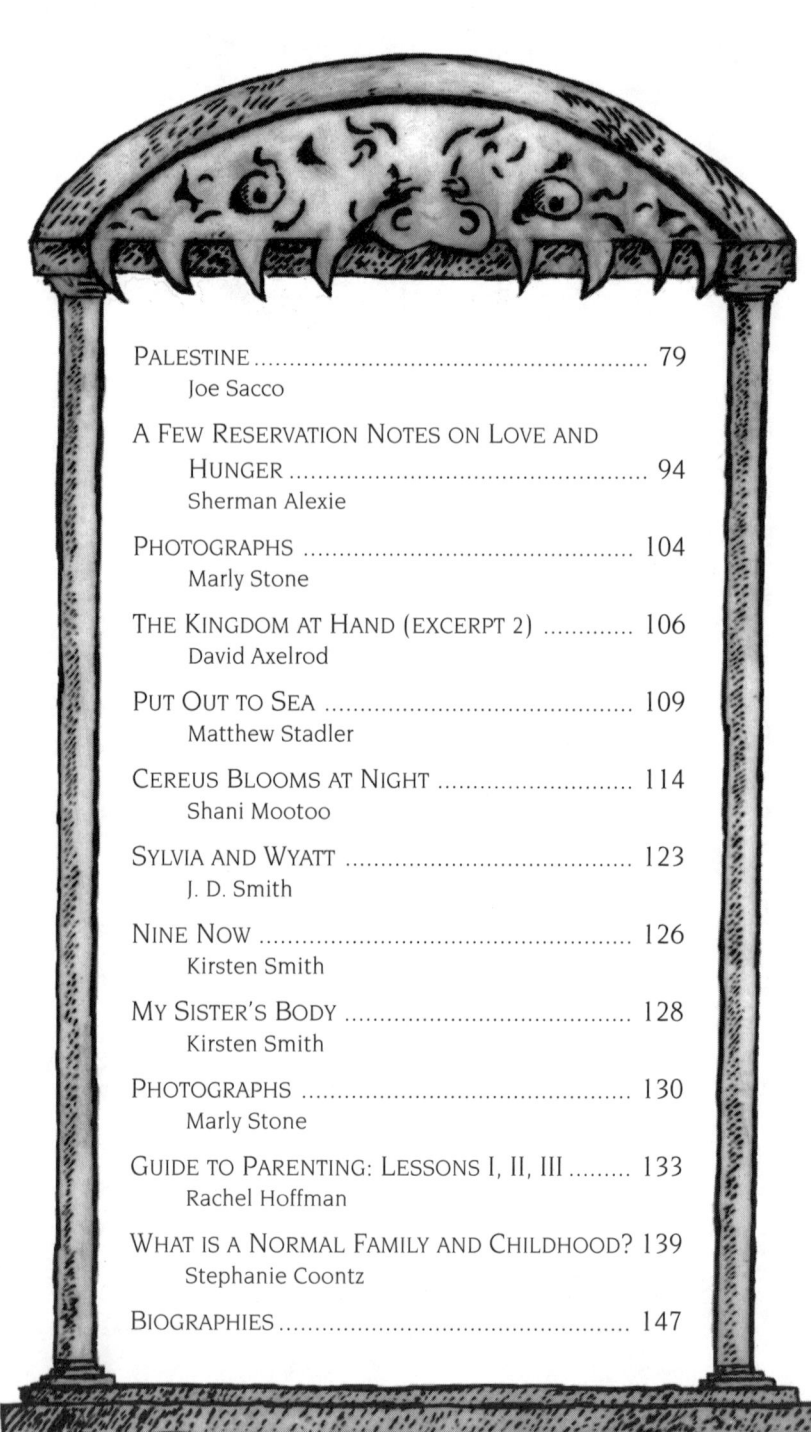

PALESTINE	79
Joe Sacco	
A FEW RESERVATION NOTES ON LOVE AND HUNGER	94
Sherman Alexie	
PHOTOGRAPHS	104
Marly Stone	
THE KINGDOM AT HAND (EXCERPT 2)	106
David Axelrod	
PUT OUT TO SEA	109
Matthew Stadler	
CEREUS BLOOMS AT NIGHT	114
Shani Mootoo	
SYLVIA AND WYATT	123
J. D. Smith	
NINE NOW	126
Kirsten Smith	
MY SISTER'S BODY	128
Kirsten Smith	
PHOTOGRAPHS	130
Marly Stone	
GUIDE TO PARENTING: LESSONS I, II, III	133
Rachel Hoffman	
WHAT IS A NORMAL FAMILY AND CHILDHOOD?	139
Stephanie Coontz	
BIOGRAPHIES	147

Foreword

As we careen through the final years of the 20th Century, into a future that seems bright and bleak in nearly equal proportion, it is proper to ask: how well are we living up to our responsibilities to our children?

This collection in the *Left Bank* series is intended to address that question, to reveal obliquely through the hum of literature and the images of art just what kind of job we're doing.

Considering the forceful cover art of Cyan Sechel, the elfish characters of Miles Inada that decorate the interior pages, and the graceful innocents in Marly Stone's photographs, a casual reader might conclude this issue is a paean to childhood.

But as the unconscious poise of childhood is all too quickly left behind, so stumbling adolescence comes to the fore: budding breasts in Kirsten Smith's "My Sister's Body," groping lovers in Shani Mootoo's "Cereus Blooms at Night," flirtation by the ant-man in J.D. Smith's "Sylvia and Wyatt," and a sketch of developing intimacy in Matthew Stadler's "Put Out to Sea," part of his upcoming book, *The Sex Offender*. Like Brian Doyle's short "Tongue Tied," in which his daughter identifies with beasts before humans, these contributions exude the joys as well as the ambiguities of growing up.

Some pieces evoke the dreams of youth — depending on how safe *your* nest was — but here also is a deviant slide down memory lane. Remember playing "house" or "doctor" where "you be" and "I'll be" imitates adult life? Juan Epple's "The Root of the Game" offered in both Spanish and English, shakes the foundations of the doll house and its ancient gender roles. Mikal Gilmore's "Life With Father" depicts a new variation of tug-of-war, played out in a family haunted by murder. It is excerpted from *Shot in the Heart*, a history of the family of Gary Gilmore (Mikal's brother), who murdered several men and was executed by firing squad in Utah. Crime writer Ann Rule's "Why Good Kids Grow Up Bad" signals an early warning of the increasing youth of criminals. Both Joe Sacco's graphic article on Palestine and Sherman Alexie's interview with his cousin about reservation life create intimate portraits of children released from childhood too soon.

Hardly kids' stuff.

Other writers expose the lies we inherit and grapple with which side of truth to tell our children. In "The Kingdom at Hand," David Axelrod weighs decadence versus romanticism in his lessons to his sons. Virginia Euwer Wolff's kids in "A Wing and a Prayer" who playact WWII in the schoolyard, discover that they can't count on adults to provide a safe world. Sallie Tisdale, in "The Happiest Place on Earth," cruises the long and perfect Disneyland myth to its reactionary creator and conclusion. Rachel Hoffman tackles Miss America, plucked eyebrows, and too-tight starter bras in the satirical "Guide to Parenting." And Neal Stephenson delivers a hilarious high-speed tale in "Deliverator" of the jobs awaiting our kids.

Stephanie Coontz's fine essay, "What is a Normal Family and Childhood?" closes the story book. She paints a tableau of parenting methods and choices for childhood from cultures around the world: caring for whichever child enters our field-of-view, fostering out children to relatives who are barren, switching roles between aunt and mother, and more. Her piece entices us with alternatives and fills us with optimism.

Heady stuff. Enjoy.

— *The editors*

Tongue Tied

Brian Doyle

My daughter Lily, once the size of a salmon, is now the size of a wood elf. She and I are bound together in many ways. In the morning we exchange food; I ladle oatmeal into her sparrow mouth and she carefully smears pears on my head. In the evening we dance in small circles and then we read. When we read she folds into me like a finger into a fist. On weekends I push her for miles in her stroller as she points to birds and dogs. When she sees a bird she says so, firmly, brooking no disagreement: "Bird!" When she sees a dog, however, she sits bolt upright and barks. Small dogs, I have discovered, back away uncertainly from barking infants.

We are also connected by language. Five of the words in her ten-word vocabulary are zoological: bird, duck, cat, dog, bug. These are strong words, brawny with consonants, and Lily uses them with abandon and confidence. Many times I've pointed out a wonder of the world — a hawk, an orange, my wife — and Lily has immediately and firmly identified it as a duck. She also does this when we read. We read the same four books every night, all of which feature the moon in a heroic capacity. There are also elves, singing flowers, cats in waistcoats. To Lily they are ducks. I have tried, in my endless wisdom, to correct her — to make her say "anthropomorphic twaddle" when the whale dons his spectacles — but she sticks with duck. I use duck a good deal myself now. It's a sturdy word, strong, forthright, firm in its resolve. I admire duck.

We connect in other ways. When I come home she

grins. In crowds she hides behind my legs. Sometimes, when she is tired, she staggers over to me and lies on my chest. I do not believe that a man can receive a greater compliment from his daughter.

Sometimes we just stare at each other. She will suddenly turn her laser gaze from a Cheerio and stare into my soul. Her eyes are green. I know who she is but I do not know her at all. She will be alive long after I'm dead. Not long ago she did not exist, and now she smears pears on my head. I love her more than I can tell you. She is my wife and me and she is God's own child. She is one of the wonders of the world. She is a duck.

Life With Father

Mikal Gilmore

> This excerpt is from Shot in the Heart, *which documents the history of the family of Gary Gilmore (Mikal's brother, executed by a firing squad in the state of Utah in 1977 for murder).*

In the years after I was born, my father kept his own photo albums, and in those books he had almost exclusively photos of me. I suppose that about sums up the reality of my early years: My father kept me. For many years — in fact, until the day he died — my father and I were our own family.

Nowhere else in life have I known such safekeeping, and such love. He would bounce me on his knee and sing "This Old Man" to me ("With a knick-knack paddywack, give the dog a bone/This old man came rolling home.") He would hold me in his arms, tickling me, calling me Tamarac. I have no idea where the name came from or what it meant, I only know it was my father's name for me when I was a child.

As I say, nowhere else did I know such love. And nowhere else have I known such loneliness and fear and guilt.

Whereas my brothers lived through vicious physical fights between my parents — all those occasions when my father battered my mother, and my brothers were made to watch — I re-

---

From Shot in the Heart, *by Mikal Gilmore. Copyright © 1994 by Mikal Gilmore; published by arrangement with Doubleday.*

member a different experience of argument. I never once saw one of my parents strike the other — or if I saw it, I simply don't remember it. I don't doubt that it happened in the earlier years, but perhaps by the time I was born my father had either learned a certain belated restraint, or was simply too old to whale the shit out of everybody *all* the time. Maybe beating my brothers was now enough to satisfy his rage.

To be sure, my parents fought, and fought frequently. Frightful, mean-spirited yelling matches that would approach the brink of violence, but never quite cross over. Instead, my mother and father would hurl terrible invectives at each other. My father would call my mother a "python spitting she-devil straight from hell" and "a crazy, crack-brained bitch." Even as a small boy — and even as somebody who often took my father's side in the end — I knew these were exceptionally awful things to call anyone, especially the person you loved. In turn, my mother would lash into my father for all the women he had loved, married and left, or at other times, she would call him a "cat-licker" — a Mormon epithet for *Catholic*. Compared to the names my father had thrown at my mother, her insults were mild, but they seemed to goad my father even more. After she made fun of his religion, he would go on a tirade about Mormons — about the evil Danites and how they did Joseph Smith's work of murder, and how Brigham Young, who was once married to twenty-seven women at the same time, had been nicknamed "Bring 'em Young." At the end of these rants, he would turn to me or my brothers, and say: "The next time you're in Salt Lake City, boys, I want you to take a look at that pompous statue they have of Brigham Young in Temple Square. I want you to look real good. If you look, you'll see that he's got his hand to the bank and his ass to the church." It was a dumb enough joke (though as it turns out, an apt description of how the statue actually stands), but it would hurt my mother deeply. She probably felt in those moments that my father was denigrating her entire past, reducing it to a petty joke. What maybe hurt more was that, to some degree, she had herself repudiated that past — her history and legacy as a Mormon, her hope of being a good Church member and enjoying access to God's care and truth — so that she could be with the man who now took such delight in belittling her.

One way or another, these arguments always seemed to mount to the crescendo of a threat. My father would threaten to leave my mother and my brothers and withdraw his support, leaving them to their own inept resources, or he would threaten to throw my mother out of the house, and make her live on the street, without money or forgiveness. I can still recall the hubristic, brutish tone with which he would taunt her, and I can still recall how her face became contorted in a pain-filled fury as my father's warnings wore on. Then he would start in on her sanity. This was probably the most malicious behavior I ever saw from him — even uglier in a way than when he hit my brothers — and it had a wicked, sure-fire effect. By calling her crazy, Frank Gilmore could provoke Bessie Gilmore to a state where she acted crazy. Her eyes would turn sharp with anger, and her face would become a strange mask that would seem in one moment both frozen and wild — as if she were containing the worst impulses a heart and mind could bear. And then she would say: "You're right — I *am* crazy. I am crazy enough to kill. Go ahead, accuse me some more, try to walk out on me. See what I'll do. I'm crazy enough that some night, when you're in your sleep, I'm going to take a sharp knife and cut your throat, and I'll laugh while your blood runs out and you gasp for the last breath of your rotten, cruel life."

Whether my mother ever meant her promises of harm or not, she was convincing in her delivery. In those instances, she was the scariest thing I have ever seen. Her eyes fixed on my father with the sort of deadliness that can only come from having been deeply wronged by the person you love most. It was in those moments, when I saw that look of menace on my mother's face, that I learned to fear anger. In particular, I learned to fear the anger of a hurt woman. Unfortunately, I also learned how to make some of that anger.

When my mother finally became the crazed creature my father accused her of being, it would break the momentum of the battle. It was as if my father felt he had won his point, but also feared what might come of his victory. He would quiet down and withdraw into his office, and my mother would be left standing there with her anger and her humiliation, in an empty room.

What made these scenes especially indelible for me was that the fights were often about the same subject: They were about me. They were about which of my parents would enjoy the custody and company of me, from day to day and place to place.

Maybe my father never fully trusted my mother with my welfare. Or maybe he simply realized he was getting older — he was nearing his late sixties during the period that I am describing here — and perhaps he simply wanted a faithful presence close to him. I suspect I might have been my father's last chance for love — a love that wouldn't refuse or betray him, or question his hard ways too much. "That man loved Mike," my mother told Larry Schiller, years later. "Really loved him. It might be the only person in the world he ever loved, but he loved that kid." And Gary himself said: "I think Mike was the only one of us that Dad ever really loved."

Whatever his reason, my father wanted me with him wherever he went. Since he traveled often for his publishing business, this meant he and I would spend a season or two in Portland, then a few months in Seattle or Tacoma, and then back and forth between these various stations. After I turned six, this meant that I would also have to go back and forth between schools, sometimes attending as many as three or four different schools in a single grade year. (With the possible exception of the first grade, I never attended any school for the entire duration of a single year until the sixth grade, the year after my father's death.)

Neither the local grammar school in Portland nor my mother thought that all this moving was such a good idea, and this is part of what became the core of contention between my parents. My father wanted me to go with him when he would travel, and my mother wanted me to stay on Johnson Creek and remain in our neighborhood school. But the argument went further. My mother also viewed my father's possessiveness of me as an attempt to keep my love to himself, and to turn me against the rest of the family. "He's my baby boy," my mother would say. "He needs to be with his mother, he needs to be close to his brothers. You're doing a horrible thing: you're turning him against me, you're making him spurn us."

I hated these fights. I remember I used to stand among my parents, spreading my arms between them, trying to keep them from hurting each other. I would beg them to stop fighting. It was like I was at the center of two monstrous, clashing forces, and if I could just make plain that I loved and wanted them both, then maybe I could stop their quarrels. Maybe then we could be a family together. Sometimes, when the bickering reached a fever pitch, my mother would say: "Let Mike choose for himself." My father would agree to this plea, but it was apparent from the way he looked at me or instructed me, that I really had no choice. "Go ahead," he would say. "Choose which of us you want to be with. Stay with your mother if you like. I'll just go away by myself, and maybe I won't come back. If you don't want me, nobody wants me." Also, by this time the arguments would invariably have reached a point where my mother had been called crazy and was hurt enough to appear that way, and the prospect of staying alone in that house with her terrified me.

I would be standing there, looking back and forth between my father and my mother, and I would almost always choose my father in these moments.

I remember well — indeed, will never be able to forget — the impact this decision would have on my mother. Her face would lose its frantic aspect and would fall into undisguised heartbreak and I would feel a horrible guilt, as if I had just hit her myself. I remember one time watching her crumble into a heap on the sofa, crying into her hands. I immediately regretted my choice, and I wanted to comfort her. I went to my mother and reached out to hold her. She flung me back, anger reddening her face, and cried: "Stay away from me. You don't love me." I ran to my father's side for protection. My mother said: "Oh Mike, I would never hurt you. I *do* love you. Come to me." But by that time I was too wary, and I would stand next to my father, my arms wrapped around his strong legs, fearing her, pitying her and wanting to be as far away from her as possible.

"That was your cross," my brother Frank told me, many years later. "I used to see you carrying that around inside you when you were little, the way you stayed away from everybody else. Many years later I used to think about that — you, stuck between them, having to choose which of them to be with. I felt for you at those times, but there wasn't anything I could say or do. There wasn't anything any of us could say or do."

This is the way I learned how to love: choosing between two loves that I could not live without, and that I could never hope to reconcile. I learned that in some ways, loving could be like killing — or that at least a certain kind of choosing was like murdering. I knew I had to hurt my parents by choosing to abandon one or the other, by being forced to declare which one I preferred over the other, which one I loved more than the other. In effect, I would kill the heart of one of them by revealing this truth, and for the most part, it was my mother's heart I had to kill. (No wonder I feared her.)

Years later, all this would feed into not only my own betrayals in love, but my misgivings about the hopefulness of the whole enterprise. Because I knew how awful it was to withhold or withdraw love, I came to fear somebody doing the same to me. I knew that to be left was to be rejected, condemned, declared unworthy. I feared, above all, somebody telling me that they didn't love me or want me or need me or want to share a life with me. In other words, I became afraid of ending up as the victim of the same sort of choices I'd had to make virtually every season of my early childhood. So sometimes I would withhold love or hedge its bets, sometimes with one too many lovers at the same time. Just as often, I would end up on the receiving end — as the one not chosen, the one left behind. It's possible, of course, that I'm leaning too much on these childhood dramas. Maybe my failures in love are simply mistakes that I alone hold the deed for. I botched the chances God gave me for love, on my own. I made for myself the unworthiness that lives in my life.

But still I have to wonder; I never thought of my parents when I kissed a woman. So why did I think of them every time I lost or failed a woman?

A few times, when my mother would threaten my father with murder in his sleep, he took her warnings seriously — or else decided to dramatize her craziness further — and folded out the couch in the living room, to make his bed for the night there. On these occasions, he kept me next to him. Either the idea was to keep me under his protection, or to insure his own safety by having me near. Before he would turn out the lights, he would take the chairs from the dining table and line them up in front of the sofa, and then he would take a heavy cord and loop it through the backs of the chairs, stringing them into a barricade. On the cord, he would hang a pair of large, rotund Chinese bells that he usually kept on his desk. That way, if my mother tried to sneak across the barrier, we would hear the bells clang. Sort of a makeshift alarm against familial murder in the dark.

Then my father would lie down, with him on the side closer to the chairs and me on the wall side, and he would fall asleep. I, however, would lie awake. I could never sleep through these nights.

I would lie there in the dark, waiting for the sound of my mother's footsteps, prepared to see the glint of a blade. I heard sounds — maybe my brothers moving around upstairs or stealing off into the night — and I'd wonder: Was it the sound of somebody coming down to kill us?

I sat up in the bed and studied the shadows of the forms about me. I could see the outline of the chairs. I could see the bells hanging on the string. But in the far reaches of the room's darkness — in the corner by the staircase, in the doorways leading to and from other rooms — I thought I could see other things. I could imagine what might be moving in that darkness. Anger and hatred and the spirit of murder moved there, in my mind's view. My mother's madness moved there. My brothers' pain. They were crouched in the shadows: forces ready to sweep down on us and stab out our lives.

Next to me my father kept sleeping, one arm sprawled out towards me, his mouth open, declaring his age: the pink, vulnerable gums that showed when he removed his dentures. In that dim light, in that insensible pose, he already looked like a dead man.

I laid back and kept listening for a movement. For a creak on the floorboards. For the rattle of the knife drawer. There are so many sounds that make so little sense in the silences of a deep night. So many that could be everything you fear the most. I would shut tight my eyes and try to force sleep to come, but it never would. Then I'd try studying the patterns on the stained wallpaper, the configurations in the lacy curtains. I think sometimes during these all night vigils, something in me went a little mad. The forms in the wallpaper, the web in the curtains, looked like little silhouettes of demons, vignettes of hell. I was afraid I'd caught some of my mother's madness. Maybe it had found its way to me, through the straits of darkness that moved in that house and in our lives. Or maybe it was merely the sleeplessness of an anxious child. I've never been a very good sleeper. Sometimes, even now, I wake up sudden. I know that something has just moved in the dark room that I am in. I feel somebody standing by my bed, and I have just heard the quick sucking sound they made, as they abruptly hold their breath. Of course, nothing is ever really there. It's just something that comes up out of my sleep, up out of me and my memory.

I would lie awake for hours on those nights, expecting my mother to come and keep her promise. When the sky began to lighten, and the room's blackness turned to the horrible dull gray of morning, I would finally feel safe enough to roll over on my side, press my feet up against my father's legs, and fade into sleep.

That's when the dreams started. When I was around five or six years old, the dreams took basically two forms. That first set of dreams had to do with things dwelling in the darkness. My father and brothers had built a wooden porch on the back of our house, and at ground level the porch had a door, which led to a storage shed for garden tools. It was a dark, dank place, with a dirt floor, and I hated it. I would never go into it. In the dreams, I would be standing in the night in front of the porch's door and it would open. I would see things spinning in the dark inside. They had fierce red eyes and sharp teeth, and they ran fast in circles, in coiling motions. I decided they were rats, and I was afraid of being devoured by them. Other times, I dreamed that something lived in our basement. In the dreams, the basement was like a dungeon — like what you might imagine from Edgar Allan Poe's descriptions of the labyrinths that ran under houses rotting from their own secrets, though I didn't associate Poe with the dreams until many years later, after reading him and taking him for my first muse. What moved in that basement in my dreams had no form. It was like a vapor, and stepping halfway down the stairs, I saw it swirl at my feet. I ran upstairs and tried to wake my family and tell them there was something coming for us from the depths of our home, something that would enter our breath in our sleep and kill us. But I could never succeed in waking them.

My other childhood dreams were more disturbing, and I have never disclosed them until now. The most common scenario of these dreams ran like this: I was a policeman or a detective — a little blond boy in a detective's suit, with a snap-brim hat and a pistol — and I was investigating a killing. I always had a partner in the dreams, and the partner was always a little girl, also with blond hair — somebody I knew I was in love with. But as the dream went along, I would realize it was I who was the killer I was seeking, and the only way to protect myself and my guilt was to kill the little girl who was my partner, whom I loved. I would kiss her, hold her close, then shoot her. I remember also — in one particularly horrible variant of this dream pattern —- that sometimes I would kill any other child or baby that I came across in the story.

I had no idea what these dreams were about when I was a child — naturally, I had no idea that dreams could be about anything — and even at this date I wouldn't profess to understand or explain them. I know that I would wake up from the dreams feeling terribly guilty, and I never told anybody about them. Sometimes, I'd go to sleep at night praying to God: "Please don't let me dream the killing dream."

But prayers never stopped the bad dreams. Never once.

Why Good Kids Grow Up Bad

Ann Rule

I have fond early memories about my summers in the Montcalm County jail and of Christmas Eves when I was tucked away in a single bunk, riveted to the wall, in a cell that smelled faintly of Pine Sol disinfectant, old layers of paint, and stale cigarette smoke. My grandfather, Chris Hansen, was the sheriff of Montcalm County, and he ran a Mom-and-Pop jail with my grandmother, Anna. The sheriff's office, the men's jail, the women's-jail-cum-mentally-ill-wing *and* my grandparents' living quarters were all located under the single roof of a big, old, dun-colored brick house.

When I spent vacations with Grandma and Grandpa, I literally went to jail. There was always a Christmas overflow too, and my cousins and I often had to sleep in the women's jail, although we were allowed to keep the cell doors open, and there were no prisoners in residence.

All of the Michigan cousins were duly imprinted by our early exposure to the criminal justice system. Nobody has yet ended up on the wrong side of the bars. One is a prosecuting attorney and another a superior court judge's clerk. We have two probation and parole officers, a clutch of lawyers — and me. After I graduated from the University of Washington, I realized my longtime ambition of becoming a police officer when I joined the Seattle Police Department.

My police career was disappointingly short-lived. I failed the civil service eye exam a year and a half later, when they discovered I was so myopic I was legally blind without my glasses. I was a social worker for a while, but I missed dealing with what had drawn me to law enforcement in the first place: an intense curiosity about why seemingly nice little children grew up to be criminals.

I always wondered "W*hy*?" and I still do. That's what led me into true crime writing. Surprising as it might sound, I still am repulsed by the gory details of murder, while I am fascinated by how "my" killers got that way. Whichever convicted felon I choose to write about, I begin by researching his or her life as far back as I can. Back to birth, and, if I'm lucky in my relentless digging into public records and family archives, even before birth. Sometimes I can find my way three or four generations up into my subjects' family trees.

I know what led me inexorably to the career I enjoy today. It all began in that Montcalm County Jail in the 1940s when my grandma cooked three meals a day for the prisoners, and I carried the tin food trays to the pantry and passed them through a slot in the wall to the prisoners. They always smiled at me and said "Thank you." They *looked* as nice as my father and my uncles were. They threw nickels out through barred windows to all the visiting cousins so we could go to town and buy ourselves ice cream cones. (At least they did until my grandfather found out.)

I drove my patient relatives crazy asking questions about prisoners. Who were they? What had they done? How could they look and seem so nice and do such bad things?

Almost half a century later, I think I have found some answers, or rather, I have drawn some parallels in the early lives of my subjects and their eventual criminal behavior. Even so, I realize the study of human criminality is in its infancy; we are learning how much we *don't* know. There is so much more to discover about why some babies grow up to become caring, empathetic, and responsible, and others mature without so much as a shadow of a conscience, crueler than any animal in the jungle.

Since human beings could form philosophical thoughts, we have questioned the importance of nature as opposed to nurture. Are we who we are because we were born that way or because of the way we were treated when we were very young? I am neither a psychiatrist or a psychologist; what I have concluded comes from a quarter of a century of reading case files, interviewing prisoners, and writing about them. And from the sociopaths I have met in my own life. Some of my wisdom is old-fashioned gut feeling, and some of it comes from experience.

Twenty years ago, I would have told you flatly that anti-social personalities were all caused by early childhood abuse, neglect, abandonment, and lack of love. In the years since, I have had my smug edges sanded off, and I am far less rigid in my pronouncements. Mothers (I am the road-weary mother of two sons, two daughters, and a foster son) have been blamed for raising bad kids for a long time. Over the decades, I have met too many mothers who were loving, caring, and who tried *everything* to help their children, and still ended up with sociopathic offspring. Being blamed only added to their pain.

I have come to believe that abuse in childhood is only one factor involved in forming aberrant personalities. Indeed, if every child who was mistreated in the first five years of life grew up to be a sociopath, the streets would be overrun with antisocial personalities, and we would be a nation in terrible trouble. I acknowledge that sometimes the nightly news makes it seem as if we are already in crisis. It isn't as bad as it seems. The vast majority of children from abusive homes stay out of trouble and out of prison. A lot of them carry emotional scars, but they pull up their socks and make new lives for themselves.

Others don't. Approximately three percent of males in our society can be deemed to be antisocial personalities, and a little over one percent of females fit within the parameters of that personality disorder too. (The terms "psychopath," "sociopath" and "antisocial personality" all mean the same thing; the latter is the more accepted in current usage.) These are the people without consciences or empathy. They will steal from us, break our hearts and never look back. They will step on our faces to win promotions at work. They tell lies with clear eyes while they smile at us. They are con men and women, always looking out for Number One. Some of them are also extremely successful entertainers, politicians, and sports figures.

I was thirteen when I met my first honest-to-goodness sociopath — at least the first one outside of jail. I'll call her "Barbara." She was fourteen, and we were both Junior Counselors at a Y.W.C.A. camp on a Michigan lake. We didn't get paid, but we got to go to camp free; in return, we were supposed to watch over our cabins full of eight and nine-year-olds whenever the senior counselors were away.

Whenever Barbara was around the Camp Director, she was nauseatingly polite and affectionate when she talked about her campers. But I knew she slipped out of her cabin every night, leaving her charges alone, while she took a canoe out to meet the boys' counselors from a camp across the lake. According to her, Barbara's life had already been fraught with near-disasters. I listened avidly as she told me stories about how many times she had saved people from fires, met movie stars, and nearly died in accidents.

"One time," she told me, "my foot was infected and it turned black and they were going to cut off my leg. Well, I told them they were going to do no such thing. When they tried to give me a shot before surgery, I jumped out of bed and ran down the hall. When I landed on my foot, the skin cracked and all the pus ran out and I was cured! And they apologized and said I had been right all along."

I believed every word, but, after a while, I began to wonder how one fourteen-year-old girl could have had all those incredible things happen. And suddenly I knew she was lying. I had never known anyone who lied like that.

She was also sleeping with her boyfriend, something unimaginable in 1950 — at least to me. Heaven knows what she was doing with the boys' camp counselors.

Nevertheless, when camp ended that year, Barbara was called into the Camp Director's office and given a check for $70, because she "had been such a wonderful and dependable counselor." That gave me pause. I was the one who never once left my campers alone, and all I got was a certificate.

Later, Barbara invited me to her home. She had been adopted by a fabulously rich couple who lived in a mansion with a curving staircase, a library, maids' quarters, buttons in the floor of every room to summon those maids, and a living room as big as our whole house. Barbara told her mother to shut up, interrupted her parents, and generally horrified me. Her mother seemed afraid of her, and she was not disciplined at all. I would have gotten a spanking.

I have often wondered where Barbara came from, and I have speculated on whatever happened to her — my first sociopath, although it would be years before I recognized what she was.

We all know sociopaths. We just don't recognize them or understand why someone we know can be so mean, and so undependable. Because most of us *do* have consciences and believe in telling the truth, we tend to think that other people are like we are.

They are not. The run-of-the-mill sociopaths are not fun to know. But they are *not* a threat to our very lives.

Fortunately, the *sadistic sociopath* is rare. But not so rare that we can ignore him/her. Think of Wesley Allan Dodd, Ted Bundy, Oregon's "Lust Killer" Jerome Brudos, Charles Manson, John Wayne Gacy. The sadistic sociopath kills for the sake of killing, and actually gets a "high" from another creature's pain. He is "addicted" to murder, just as a drug user is addicted to heroin or cocaine; it takes more and more of the "substance" to give the sadistic killer the high he got the first time, so his crimes escalate and become more intricate.

The blacker the "soul" inside, however, the smoother and more charismatic the exterior. I worked beside Ted Bundy (who admitted to three dozen murders and is suspected of killing over 100 young women) at Seattle's Crisis Clinic all night long every Sunday and Tuesday for a year. Together, we saved lives. He walked me to my car in the dark at dawn and warned me to be careful on the way home because he didn't want "anything bad to happen to me."

I never spotted one vestige of aberrance in Ted, even though I had a police, psychology, and social work background. He did tell me about how he learned that he had been born an illegitimate baby. He described how he discovered that his "big sister" was really his mother when he returned to his Vermont birthplace at the age of 22. At least he told me the version of his life he wanted me to believe. He told me his father/grandfather was a warm Santa Claus-like man; I didn't learn until the week Ted Bundy was executed that his Grandfather Cowell had been a man with a maniacal temper who allegedly terrified his entire household, including Ted, during the first five years of his life. The old man reportedly collected violent pornography, was cruel to animals, and threw his daughters down the stairs.

Was he a role model? Was the fear he created causative? Or had he handed down "violent genes?" Or all three?

Acknowledging that there are gradations of sociopathy — from psychopathic liars who will tell you anything to get attention to sadistic serial killers — let's go back to figuring out how sociopaths got that way.

If you look at newborn babies in a hospital nursery, they are all adorable and pink and sweet smelling, but even at birth they have distinctive little personalities. No adult has had a chance to affect them one way or the other, either by loving and cuddling or by neglecting them. Even so, some babies are laid-back and can sleep right through loud noises. Others startle easily, are tense, and cry most of the time. Ask any mother of more than one child, and she will tell you that they are all different.

Some babies snuggle and love to be held; some stiffen and pull back. I swear some babies have senses of humor and chortle with delight, while others view the world with suspicion. I have come to believe that there well may be a genetic predisposition to violence, just as there are genetic predispositions to athletic prowess, musical talent, asthma, myopia, hair and eye color, and on and on.

If the genetic tendency toward violence is not nourished and encouraged, if a child is born into a home where he will receive extra attention, calm, undemanding love, and a sense of belonging, that dangerous little seed will never flourish. But, if we look at an infant with an inborn "talent" for violence, who is raised haphazardly in a home with cold, abusive, and undependable parent figures, we may very well see that violence balloon and grow until there is no treatment that can cure it.

A few months ago, I was on a book tour and found myself on the same television talk show with an expert on human behavior whom I have admired for a long time: Dr. Robert Hare, a Vancouver, British Columbia, forensic psychiatrist, and author of *Without Conscience: The Deadly Mystery of the Psychopath* (Simon & Schuster, 1993). Between us, we have met dozens of sadistic sociopaths, perhaps a somewhat dubious distinction to share. We talked about the possibility that there might be a *physiological* tendency toward criminal and conscienceless behavior. I was intrigued when Dr. Hare told me that new studies of MRI (Magnetic Resonance Imaging) images of human brains — belonging to both normal and sociopathic subjects — showed entirely different results. MRIs show brain activity in different colors. To put it simplistically, red for hot, blue for cold, and all shadings in between.

If there were not some basic physical difference between the brains of sociopaths and those of conscience-driven people, why would their MRIs be so different?

"Do you think they were born that way?" I asked Dr. Hare.

He paused. "Maybe. But think of this — what if a very young child is so abused that his brain actually changes?"

That was, quite probably, the first time I could imagine nature and nurture intermingling to actually *change* a child physically so much that a grotesque and potentially tragic result was created: an antisocial personality. Of all the theories I have ever explored, this one made the most sense. I have always refused to believe in the bad-seed-no-hope theory. I don't think any baby is destined to grow up to be evil. I *do* think that the combination of a baby who is highly intelligent, highly sensitive, and who may well have inherited a tendency to be aggressive and volatile, *and* has a miserable home life can spawn a headline-making monster.

Picture the newborn Ted Bundy. Because his mother was bewildered and frightened, she wasn't sure what to do with him. She left him at the Elizabeth Lund Home for Unwed Mothers for four months, seesawing between putting him out for adoption and taking him home to her parents' house. On some level, I believe he *knew* he was not wanted. For those essential first months when he should have been bonding with a mother-figure, Ted lay alone in his crib. He was fed and changed by an impersonal staff; no one had time to cuddle him or talk to him.

He knew. I think the rage in Ted Bundy began to grow before he was even six months old.

Most children begin to figure out at about the age of three that other creatures hurt, too. They see that puppies yelp when their tails are pulled, and that sisters cry when they are bitten. And they feel sorry for another's pain. The emerging sociopath is so busy trying to survive in a home barren of love that he has no time or energy to grow a conscience. He cannot fight back; he is too little to do battle with the adults who control his life. But neither does he grow a conscience. With every year that passes, he becomes more alienated from the feelings of others. He knows the difference between right and wrong, but it doesn't matter.

He is special. Above all, he must survive. And whatever it takes to stay alive and to feel pleasure, he — or she — will do that. At some point, he acclimates to the only life he knows. He has no desire at all to change.

We cannot transplant a working conscience into a full-blown sociopath who may be eleven or twelve or fourteen. It would be easier to jack up a ten-story brick building constructed on a flimsy foundation, and insert a solid first floor. It is too late.

Far too late.

I fear we are heading for chilling statistics involving younger and younger felons. Antisocial children seem to be acting out sooner than they did in earlier generations. Sadly, nine-year-old killers are showing up more and more often on the five o'clock news. And violent death is integral to television programming. By the time children are ten, they have seen thousands of murders on the little screen. As an author, I oppose censorship. As a human being, I urge producers to consider what enormous impact they have on young minds and self-edit accordingly.

Today television often replaces human contact. When I was a child, I had only one friend whose parents were divorced and whose mother had to work. My children have only one or two friends whose parents have *not* divorced at least once. Fifty years ago — even twenty years ago — families were less mobile than they are now. If there was not a parent home to take care of children, there was usually a grandmother or an aunt. Now, that loving, extended-family member might well be living two or three thousand miles away from the child. Every child needs at least one *champion*, one person who lets them know they are special. It might be a relative, a teacher, a coach, a minister. When there is no one at all, there is fertile soil for sociopaths to grow.

If I had a magic wand and I could wave it over budget planners in Washington, D.C., I would allocate more funds to child care, lessons on parenting, early childhood education, counseling, and housing for homeless mothers. The only way to keep good kids from growing up "bad" is to take care of the babies. Now.

Excerpt #1 from

The Kingdom at Hand

David Axelrod

An old man wants to know if my generation
hasn't given up the Romantic spirit
of his youth, chosen to embrace decadence?
But he doesn't really blame us for that,
"What kind of world did we leave for you?"
And before I can answer, he wants to know,
"Do you have children? What do you tell them
the world was like when you were still young?"

He expects me to gripe with him, as though
I'd tell my children something glib like:
Give up! Your planet is dying. As though
maybe I'd keep them up at night listening
to the weeping that travels from city to city
along high voltage lines that hiss
in humid air, leaking kilowatts of defeat.

And what if everything is weeping:
fields of corn, quarried granite, books
that absolutely refuse to look us in the face,
refrigerators weeping into narrow drains,
dentures that do and don't fit, thrushes,
maples, priceless grain rotting in fields,
or haircuts, heaps of junk tires, defiant
people peering at us from underpasses,
even millionaires with excellent hygiene,
all as good as dead, all weeping?

It's merely apocalyptic sorrow, so much waste,
le fin de siècle, the millennial nightmare.
It's the sense of something big coming our way
after years without rain, wind worrying pines,
driving ahead of it the scent of fires,
flocks of panicked birds, and by evening,
the ocean, the reek of salt, fish and storm.

Something is ending now, but it's more than
the 20th century, or Europe, more than theory,
justice, or law — those dying old men
whose hands flutter like moths at windowsills.
And it's far more than you or I at five AM,
opening boxes of old LPs, discovering the *Eroica*
has vanished, Beethoven's scratchy music
gone out of the black, spiraling grooves.

And what remains? Only a puffed-up
Romantic portrait of Napoleon, unhorsed,
a frightened little emperor, retreating from
the ferocious sound of a composer's will.

It's all gone wrong, and gone wrong again!
Bankers and lawyers occupy the Commune.
The day opens and closes and opens
its ten thousand eyes, the marbled sky
dropping heaps of gold in weeds at my feet,
gold like long hair tossed down from the Tower,
though what resides up there is bitter,
and the Host turns our tongues to char.

So what do I tell my young sons about
the glorious past, the infinite landscape
of possibilities just around the corner?
Should I tell them there's no such thing
as gravity, no drag chain, no weight,
no limitations to desire? Or should I
show them how evil is streamlined, precise,
pure, and above all, profitable, source
of every comfort but satisfaction?

The Deliverator

Neal Stephenson

The Deliverator belongs to an elite order, a hallowed subcategory. He's got esprit up to here. Right now, he is preparing to carry out his third mission of the night. His uniform is black as activated charcoal, filtering the very light out of the air. A bullet will bounce off its arachnofiber weave like a wren hitting a patio door, but excess perspiration wafts through it like a breeze through a freshly napalmed forest. Where his body has bony extremities, the suit has sintered armorgel: feels like gritty jello, protects like a stack of telephone books.

The Deliverator's car has enough potential energy packed into its batteries to fire a pound of bacon into the Asteroid Belt. Unlike a bimbo box or a Burb beater, the Deliverator's car unloads that power through gaping, gleaming, polished sphincters. When the Deliverator puts the hammer down, shit happens. You want to talk contact patches? Your car's tires have tiny contact patches, talk to the asphalt in four places the size of your tongue. The Deliverator's car has big sticky tires with contact patches the size of a fat lady's thighs. The Deliverator is in touch with the road, starts like a bad day, stops on a peseta.

From *Snow Crash* by Neal Stephenson. Copyright © 1992 by Neal Stephenson. Reprinted by permission of Bantam Books, a division of Bantam Doubleday Dell Publishing Group, Inc. All Rights Reserved.

Why is the Deliverator so equipped? Because people rely on him. He is a roll model. This is America. People do whatever the fuck they feel like doing, you got a problem with that? Because they have a right to. And because they have guns and no one can fucking stop them. As a result, this country has one of the worst economies in the world. When it gets down to it — talking trade balances here — once we've brain-drained all our technology into other countries, once things have evened out, they're making cars in Bolivia and microwave ovens in Tadzhikistan and selling them here — once our edge in natural resources has been made irrelevant by giant Hong Kong ships and dirigibles that can ship North Dakota all the way to New Zealand for a nickel — once the Invisible Hand has taken all those historical inequities and smeared them out into a broad global layer of what a Pakistani brickmaker would consider to be prosperity — y'know what? There's only four things we do better than anyone else

        music
        movies
        microcode (software)
        high-speed pizza delivery

The Deliverator used to make software. Still does, sometimes. But if life were a mellow elementary school run by well-meaning education Ph.D.s, the Deliverator's report card would say: "Hiro is *so* bright and creative but needs to work harder on his cooperation skills."

So now he has this other job. No brightness or creativity involved — but no cooperation either. Just a single principle: The Deliverator stands tall, your pie in thirty minutes or you can have it free, shoot the driver, take his car, file a class-action suit. The Deliverator has been working this job for six months, a rich and lengthy tenure by his standards, and has never delivered a pizza in more than twenty-one minutes.

Oh, they used to argue over times, many corporate driver-years lost to it: homeowners, red-faced and sweaty with their own lies, stinking of Old Spice and job-related stress, standing in their glowing yellow doorways brandishing their Seikos and waving at the clock over the kitchen sink, I swear, can't you guys tell time?

Didn't happen anymore. Pizza delivery a major industry. A managed industry. People went to CosaNostra Pizza University four years just to learn it. Came in its doors unable to write an English sentence, from Abkhazia, Rwanda, Guanajuato, South Jersey, and came out knowing more about pizza than a Bedouin knows about sand. And they had studied this problem. Graphed the frequency of doorway delivery-time disputes. Wired the early Deliverators to record, then analyze, the debating tactics, the voice-stress histograms, the distinctive grammatical structures employed by white middle-class Type A Burbclave occupants who against all logic had decided that this was the place to take their personal Custerian stand against all that was stale and deadening in their lives: they were going to lie, or delude themselves, about the time of their phone call and get themselves a free pizza; no, they deserved a free pizza along with their life, liberty, and pursuit of whatever, it was fucking inalienable.

The analysts at CosaNostra Pizza University concluded that it was just human nature and you couldn't fix it, and so they went for a quick cheap technical fix: smart boxes. The pizza box is a plastic carapace now, corrugated for stiffness, a little LED readout glowing on the side, telling the Deliverator how many trade imbalance-producing minutes have ticked away since the fateful phone call. There are chips and stuff in there. The pizzas rest, a short stack of them, in slots behind the Deliverator's head. Each pizza glides into a slot like a circuit board into a computer, clicks into place as the smart box interfaces with the onboard system of the Deliverator's car. The address of the caller has already been inferred from his phone number and poured into the smart box's built-in RAM. From there it is communicated to the car, which computes and projects the optimal route on a heads-up display, a glowing colored map traced out against the windshield so that the Deliverator does not even have to glance down.

If the thirty-minute deadline expires, news of the disaster is flashed to CosaNostra Pizza Headquarters and relayed from there to Uncle Enzo himself — the Sicilian Colonel Sanders, the Andy Griffith of Bensonhurst, the straight razor-swinging figment of many a Deliverator's nightmares, the Capo and prime figurehead of CosaNostra Pizza, Incorporated — who will be on the phone to the customer within five minutes, apologizing profusely. The next day, Uncle Enzo will land on the customer's yard in a jet helicopter and apologize some more and give him a free trip to Italy — all he has to do is sign a bunch of releases that make him a public figure and spokesperson for CosaNostra Pizza and basically end his private life as he knows it.

The Deliverator does not know for sure what happens to the driver in such cases, but he has heard some rumors. Most pizza deliveries happen in the evening hours, which Uncle Enzo considers to be his private time. And how would you feel if you had to interrupt dinner with your family in order to call some obstreperous dork in a Burbclave and grovel for a late fucking pizza? Uncle Enzo has not put in fifty years serving his family and his country so that, at the age when most are playing golf and bobbling their granddaughters, he can get out of the bathtub dripping wet and lie down and kiss the feet of some sixteen-year-old skate punk whose pepperoni was thirty-one minutes in coming. Oh, God. It makes the Deliverator breathe a little shallower just to think of the idea.

But he wouldn't drive for CosaNostra Pizza any other way. You know why? Because there's something about having your life on the line. It's like being a kamikaze pilot. Your mind is clear. Other people — store clerks, burger flippers, software engineers, the whole vocabulary of meaningless jobs that make up Life in America — other people just rely on plain old competition. Better flip your burgers or debug your subroutines faster and better than your high school classmate two blocks down the strip is flipping or debugging, because we're in competition with those guys, and people notice these things.

What a fucking rat race that is. CosaNostra Pizza doesn't have any competition. Competition goes against the Mafia ethic. You don't work harder because you're competing against some identical operation down the street. You work harder because everything is on the line. Your name, your honor, your family, your life. Those burger flippers might have a better life expectancy — but what kind of life is it anyway, you have to ask yourself. That's why nobody, not even the Nipponese, can move pizzas faster than CosaNostra. The Deliverator is proud to wear the uniform, proud to drive the car, proud to march up the front walks of innumerable Burbclave homes, a grim vision in ninja black, a pizza on his shoulder, red LED digits blazing proud numbers into the night: 12:32 or 15:15 or the occasional 20:43.

CosaNostra Pizza #3569 is on Vista Road just down from Kings Park Mall. Vista Road used to belong to the State of California and now is called Fairlanes, Inc. Rte. CSV-5. Its main competition used to be a U.S. highway and is now called Cruiseways, Inc. Rte. Cal-12. Farther up the Valley, the two competing highways actually cross. Once there had been bitter disputes, the intersection closed by sporadic sniper fire. Finally, a big developer bought the entire intersection and turned it into a drive-through mall. Now the roads just feed into a parking system — not a lot, not a ramp, but a system — and lose their identity. Getting through the intersection involves tracing paths through the parking system, many braided filaments of direction like the Ho Chi Minh trail. CSV-5 has better throughput, but Cal-12 has better pavement. That is typical — Fairlanes roads emphasize getting you there, for Type A drivers, and Cruiseways emphasize the enjoyment of the ride, for Type B drivers.

The Deliverator is a Type A driver with rabies. He is zeroing in on his home base, CosaNostra Pizza #3569, cranking up the left lane of CSV-5 at a hundred and twenty kilometers. His car is an invisible black lozenge, just a dark place that reflects the tunnel of franchise signs — the loglo. A row of orange lights burbles and churns across the front, where the grille would be if this were an air-breathing car. The orange light looks like a gasoline fire. It comes in through people's rear windows, bounces off their rearview mirrors, projects a fiery mask across their eyes, reaches into their subconscious, and unearths terrible fears of being pinned, fully conscious, under a detonating gas tank, makes them want to pull over and let the Deliverator overtake them in his black chariot of pepperoni fire.

The loglo, overhead, marking out CSV-5 in twin contrails, is a body of electrical light made of innumerable cells, each cell designed in Manhattan by imageers who make more for designing a single logo than a Deliverator will make in his entire lifetime. Despite their efforts to stand out, they all smear together, especially at a hundred and twenty kilometers per hour. Still, it is easy to see CosaNostra Pizza #3569 because of the billboard, which is wide and tall even by current inflated standards. In fact, the squat franchise itself looks like nothing more than a low-slung base for the great aramid fiber pillars that thrust the billboard up into the trademark firmament. Marca Registrada, baby.

The billboard is a classic, a chestnut, not a figment of some fleeting Mafia promotional campaign. It is a statement, a monument built to endure. Simple and dignified. It shows Uncle Enzo in one of his spiffy Italian suits. The pinstripes glint and flex like sinews. The pocket square is luminous. His hair is perfect, slicked back with something that never comes off, each strand cut off straight and square at the end by Uncle Enzo's cousin, Art the Barber, who runs the second-largest chain of low-end haircutting establishments in the world. Uncle Enzo is standing there, not exactly smiling, an avuncular glint in his eye for sure, not posing like a model but standing there like your uncle would, and it says

The Mafia
you've got a friend in The Family!
paid for by the Our Thing Foundation

The billboard serves as the Deliverator's polestar. He knows that when he gets to the place on CSV-5 where the bottom corner of the billboard is obscured by the pseudo-Gothic stained-glass arches of the local Reverend Wayne's Pearly Gates franchise, it's time for him to get over into the right lanes where the retards and the bimbo boxes poke along, random, indecisive, looking at each passing franchise's driveway like they don't know if it's a promise or a threat.

He cuts off a bimbo box — a family minivan — veers past the Buy 'n' Fly that is next door, and pulls into CosaNostra Pizza #3569. Those big fat contact patches complain, squeal a little bit, but they hold on to the patented Fairlanes, Inc. high-traction pavement and guide him into the chute. No other Deliverators are waiting in the chute. That is good, that means high turnover for him, fast action, keep moving that 'za. As he scrunches to a stop, the electromechanical hatch on the flank of his car is already opening to reveal his empty pizza slots, the door clicking and folding back in on itself like the wing of a beetle. The slots are waiting. Waiting for hot pizza.

And waiting. The Deliverator honks his horn. This is not a nominal outcome.

Window slides open. That should never happen. You can look at the three-ring binder from CosaNostra Pizza University, cross-reference the citation for *window, chute, dispatcher's*, and it will give you all the procedures for that window — and it should never be opened. Unless something has gone wrong.

The window slides open and — you sitting down? — *smoke* comes out of it. The Deliverator hears a discordant beetling over the metal hurricane of his sound system and realizes that it is a smoke alarm, coming from inside the franchise.

Mute button on the stereo. Oppressive silence — his eardrums uncringe — the window is buzzing with the cry of the smoke alarm. The car idles, waiting. The hatch has been open too long, atmospheric pollutants are congealing on the electrical contacts in the back of the pizza slots, he'll have to clean them ahead of schedule, everything is going exactly the way it shouldn't go in the three-ring binder that spells out all the rhythms of the pizza universe.

Inside, a football-shaped Abkhazian man is running to and fro, holding a three-ring binder open, using his spare tire as a ledge to keep it from collapsing shut; he runs with the gait of a man carrying an egg on a spoon. He is shouting in the Abkhazian dialect; all the people who run CosaNostra pizza franchises in this part of the Valley are Abkhazian immigrants.

The Deliverator holds the horn button down. The Abkhazian

manager comes to the window. He is supposed to use the intercom to talk to drivers, he could say anything he wanted and it would be piped straight into the Deliverator's car, but no, he has to talk face to face, like the Deliverator is some kind of fucking ox cart driver. He is red-faced, sweating, his eyes roll as he tries to think of the English words.

"A fire, a little one," he says.

The Deliverator says nothing. Because he knows that all of this is going onto videotape. The tape is being pipelined, as it happens, to CosaNostra Pizza University, where it will be analyzed in a pizza management science laboratory. It will be shown to Pizza University students, perhaps to the very students who will replace this man when he gets fired, as a textbook example of how to screw up your life.

"New employee — put his dinner in the microwave — had foil in it — boom!" the manager says.

Abkhazia had been part of the Soviet fucking Union. A new immigrant from Abkhazia trying to operate a microwave was like a deep-sea tube worm doing brain surgery. Where did they get these guys? Weren't there any Americans who could bake a fucking pizza?

"Just give me one pie," the Deliverator says.

Talking about pies snaps the guy into the current century. He gets a grip. He slams the window shut, strangling the relentless keening of the smoke alarm.

A Nipponese robot arm shoves the pizza out and into the top slot. The hatch folds shut to protect it.

As the Deliverator is pulling out of the chute, building up speed, checking the address that is flashed across his windshield, deciding whether to turn right or left, it happens. His stereo cuts out again on command of the onboard system. The cockpit lights go red. *Red.* A repetitive buzzer begins to sound. The LED readout on his windshield, which echoes the one on the pizza box, flashes up: 20:00.

They have just given the Deliverator a twenty-minute-old pizza. He checks the address; it is twelve miles away.

The Deliverator lets out an involuntary roar and puts the hammer down. His emotions tell him to go back and kill that manager, get his swords out of the trunk, dive in through the little sliding window like a ninja, track him down through the moiling chaos of the microwaved franchise and confront him in a climactic thick-crust apocalypse. But he thinks the same thing when someone cuts him off on the freeway, and he's never done it — yet.

He can handle this. This is doable. He cranks up the orange warning lights to maximum brilliance, puts his headlights on autoflash. He overrides the warning buzzer, jams the stereo over to Taxiscan, which cruises all the taxi-driver frequencies listening for interesting traffic. Can't understand a fucking word. You could buy tapes, learn-while-you-drive, and learn to speak Taxilinga. It was essential, to get a job in that business. They said it was based on English but not one word in a hundred was recognizable. Still, you could get an idea. If there was trouble on this road, they'd be babbling about it in Taxilinga, give him some warning, let him take an alternate route so he wouldn't get

he grips the wheel
stuck in traffic
his eyes get big, he can feel the pressure driving them back into his skull
or caught behind a mobile home
his bladder is very full
and deliver the pizza
oh, God oh, God
late
22:06 hangs on the windshield; all he can see, all he can think about is 30:01.

The taxi drivers are buzzing about something. Taxilinga is mellifluous babble with a few harsh foreign sounds, like butter spiced with broken glass. He keeps hearing "fare." They are always jabbering about their fucking fares. Big deal. What happens if you deliver your fare *late* you don't get as much of a tip? Big deal.

Big slowdown at the intersection of CSV-5 and Oahu Road, per usual, only way to avoid it is to cut through The Mews at Windsor Heights.

TMAWHs all have the same layout. When creating a new Burbclave, TMAWH Development Corporation will chop down any mountain ranges and divert the course of any mighty rivers that threaten to interrupt this street plan ergonomically designed to encourage driving safety. A Deliverator can go into a Mews at Windsor Heights anywhere from Fairbanks to Yaroslavl to the Shenzhen special economic zone and find his way around.

But once you've delivered a pie to every single house in a TMAWH a few times, you get to know its little secrets. The Deliverator is such a man. He knows that in a standard TMAWH there is only one yard — one yard — that prevents you from driving straight in one entrance, across the Burbclave, and out the other. If you are squeamish about driving on grass, it might take you ten minutes to meander through TMAWH. But if you have the balls to lay tracks across that one yard, you have a straight shot through the center.

The Deliverator knows that yard. He has delivered pizzas there. He has looked at it, scoped it out, memorized the location of the shed and the picnic table, can find them even in the dark — knows that if it ever came to this, a twenty-three-minute pizza, miles to go, and a slowdown at CSV-5 and Oahu — he could enter The Mews at Windsor Heights (his electronic delivery-man's visa would raise the gate automatically), scream down Heritage Boulevard, rip the turn onto Strawbridge Place (ignoring the DEAD END sign and the speed limit and the CHILDREN PLAYING ideograms that are strung so liberally throughout TMAWH), thrash the speed bumps with his mighty radials, blast up the driveway of Number 15 Strawbridge Circle, cut a hard left around the backyard shed, careen into the backyard of Number 84 Mayapple Place, avoid its picnic table (tricky), get into their driveway and out onto Mayapple, which takes him to Bellewoode Valley Road, which runs straight to the exit of the Burbclave. TMAWH security police might be waiting for him at the exit, but their STDs, Severe Tire Damage devices, only point one way — they can keep people out, but not keep them in.

This car can go so fucking fast that if a cop took a bite of a doughnut as the Deliverator was entering Heritage Boulevard, he probably wouldn't be able to swallow it until about the time the Deliverator was shrieking out onto Oahu.

Thunk. And more red lights come up on the windshield: the perimeter security of the Deliverator's vehicle has been breached.

No. It can't be.

Someone is shadowing him. Right off his left flank. A person on a skateboard, rolling down the highway right behind him, just as he is laying in his approach vectors to Heritage Boulevard.

The Deliverator, in his distracted state, has allowed himself to get pooned. As in harpooned. It is a big round padded electromagnet on the end of an arachnofiber cable. It has just thunked onto the back of the Deliverator's car, and stuck. Ten feet behind him, the owner of this cursed device is surfing, taking him for a ride, skateboarding along like a water skier behind a boat.

In the rearview, flashes of orange and blue. The parasite is not just a punk out having a good time. It is a businessman making money. The orange and blue coverall, bulging all over with sintered armorgel padding, is the uniform of a Kourier. A Kourier from RadiKS, Radikal Kourier Systems. Like a bicycle messenger, but a hundred times more irritating because they don't pedal under their own power — they just latch on and slow you down.

Naturally. The Deliverator was in a hurry, flashing his lights, squealing his contact patches. The fastest thing on the road. Naturally, the Kourier would choose him to latch onto.

No need to get rattled. With the shortcut through TMAWH, he will have plenty of time. He passes a slower car in the middle lane, then cuts right in front of him. The Kourier will have to unpoon or else be slammed sideways into the slower vehicle.

Done. The Kourier isn't ten feet behind him anymore — he is right there, peering in the rear window. Anticipating the maneuver, the Kourier reeled in his cord, which is attached to a handle with a power reel in it, and is now right on top of the pizza mobile, the front wheel of his skateboard actually underneath the Deliverator's rear bumper.

An orange-and-blue-gloved hand reaches forward, a transparent sheet of plastic draped over it, and slaps his driver's side window. The Deliverator has just been stickered. The sticker is a foot across and reads, in big orange block letters, printed backward so that he can read it from the inside.

THAT WAS STALE

He almost misses the turnoff for The Mews at Windsor Heights. He has to jam the brakes, let traffic clear, cut across the curb lane to enter the Burbclave. The border post is well lighted, the customs agents ready to frisk all comers — cavity-search them if they are the wrong kind of people — but the gate flies open as if by magic as the security system senses that this is a CosaNostra Pizza vehicle, just making a delivery, sir. And as he goes through, the Kourier — that tick on his ass — waves to the border police! What a prick! Like he comes in here all the time!

He probably does come in here all the time. Picking up important shit for important TMAWH people, delivering it to other FOQNEs, Franchise-Organized Quasi-National Entities, getting it through customs. That's what Kouriers do. Still.

He's going too slow, lost all his momentum, his timing is off. Where's the Kourier? Ah, reeled out some line, is following behind again. The Deliverator knows that this jerk is in for a big surprise. Can he stay on his fucking skateboard while he's being hauled over the flattened remains of some kid's plastic tricycle at a hundred kilometers? We're going to find out.

The Kourier leans back — the Deliverator can't help watching in the rearview — leans back like a water skier, pushes off against his board, and swings around beside him, now traveling abreast with him up Heritage Boulevard and *slap* another sticker goes up, this one on the windshield! It says

SMOOTH MOVE, EX-LAX

The Deliverator has heard of these stickers. It takes hours to get them off. Have to take the car into a detailing place, pay trillions of dollars. The Deliverator has two things on his agenda now: He is going to shake this street scum, whatever it takes, and deliver the fucking pizza all in the space of

24:23

the next five minutes and thirty-seven seconds.

This is it — got to pay more attention to the road — he swings into the side street, no warning, hoping maybe to whipsaw the Kourier into the street sign on the corner. Doesn't work. The smart ones watch your front tires, they see when you're turning, can't surprise them. Down Strawbridge Place! It seems so long, longer than he remembered — natural when you're in a hurry. Sees the glint of cars up ahead, cars parked sideways to the road — these must be parked in the circle. And there's the house. Light blue vinyl clapboard two-story with one-story garage to the side. He makes that driveway the center of his universe, puts the Kourier out of his mind, tries not to think about Uncle Enzo.

The slope of the driveway slams his front suspension halfway up into the engine compartment, but that's what suspensions are for. He evades the car in the driveway — must have visitors tonight, didn't remember that these people drove a Lexus — cuts through the hedge, into the side yard, looks for that shed, that shed he absolutely must not run into

it's not there, they took it down

next problem, the picnic table in the next yard

hang on, there's a fence, when did they put up a fence?

This is no time to put on the brakes. Got to build up some speed, knock it down without blowing all this momentum. It's just a four-foot wooden thing.

The fence goes down easy, he loses maybe ten percent of his speed. But strangely, it looked like an *old* fence, maybe he made a wrong turn somewhere — he realizes, as he catapults into an empty backyard swimming pool.

If it had been full of water, that wouldn't have been so bad, maybe the car would have been saved, he wouldn't owe CosaNostra Pizza a new car. But no, he does a Stuka into the far wall of the pool, it sounds more like an explosion than a crash. The airbag inflates, comes back down a second later like a curtain revealing the structure of his new life: he is stuck in a dead car in an empty pool in a TMAWH, the sirens of the Burbclave's security police are approaching, and there's a pizza behind his head, resting there like the blade of a guillotine, with 25:17 on it.

"Where's it going?" someone says. A woman.

He looks up through the distorted frame of the window, now rimmed with a fractal pattern of crystallized safety glass. It is the Kourier talking to him. The Kourier is not a man, it is a young woman. A fucking teenaged girl. She is pristine, unhurt. She has skated right down into the pool, she's now oscillating back and forth from one side of the pool to the other, skating up one bank, almost to the lip, turning around, skating down and across and up the opposite side. She is holding her poon in her right hand, the electromagnet reeled up against the handle so it looks like some kind of a strange wide-angle intergalactic death ray. Her chest glitters like a general's with a hundred little ribbons and medals, except each rectangle is not a ribbon, it is a bar code. A bar code with an ID number that gets her into a different business, highway, or FOQNE.

"Yo!" she says. "Where's the pizza going?"

He's going to die and she's *gamboling*.

"White Columns. 5 Oglethorpe Circle," he says.

"I can do that. Open the hatch."

His heart expands to twice its normal size. Tears come to his eyes. He may live. He presses a button and the hatch opens.

On her next orbit across the bottom of the pool, the Kourier yanks the pizza out of its slot. The Deliverator winces, imagining the garlicky topping accordioning into the back wall of the box. Then she puts it sideways under her arm. It's more than a Deliverator can stand to watch.

But she'll get it there. Uncle Enzo doesn't have to apologize for ugly, ruined, cold pizzas, just late ones.

"Hey," he says, "take this."

The Deliverator sticks his black-clad arm out the shattered window. A white rectangle glows in the dim backyard light: a business card. The Kourier snatches it from him on her next orbit, reads it. It says

> # HIRO PROTAGONIST
> *Last of the freelance hackers*
> *Greatest sword fighter in the world*
> *Stringer, Central Intelligence Corporation*
> *Specializing in software-related intel*
> *(music, movies & microcode)*

On the back is gibberish explaining how he may be reached: a telephone number. A universal voice phone locator code. A P.O. box. His address on half a dozen electronic communications nets. And an address in the Metaverse.

"Stupid name," she says, shoving the card into one of a hundred little pockets on her coverall.

"But you'll never forget it," Hiro says.

"If you're a hacker…"

"How come I'm delivering pizzas?"

"Right."

"Because I'm a freelance hacker. Look, whatever your name is — I owe you one."

"Name's Y.T.," she says, shoving at the pool a few times with one foot, building up more energy. She flies out of the pool as if catapulted, and she's gone. The smartwheels of her skateboard, many, many spokes extending and retracting to fit the shape of the ground, take her across the lawn like a pat of butter skidding across hot Teflon.

Photographs

Marly Stone

> Marly Stone wrote the following introduction for a gallery show in 1992. Not all these photographs (placed in three sets throughout the book) were in that exhibit, but her thoughts are most appropriate here.

The way I work is to follow my instincts. I don't think about what the inspiration means. I just let it come through. In this way I get life lessons.

And so it goes with my photography. The photos on exhibit were shot during my stay in Pietra Santa, Italy, where I want to sculpt with sculptors from all over the globe and in the *laboratorios* (studios) of artisans whose forefathers had been perfecting the craft since before Michelangelo. As a photographer, I couldn't resist the ancient beauty of the *laboratorios* where I was working. I found some beautiful sculptresses and persuaded them to model for me. Then I watched the light for months so I could shoot at the perfect moments. By the end of my first three-month stay, I almost completed one sculpture and got a good start on my photographic series, which, it became clear to me, was making classical work with a contemporary medium. This theme has been in my photography for years, only now, I was in exactly the right environment. The questions I began dealing with were "What is time?", "Have people changed through time?", and "What is real?"

Surrounded by all those buildings and sculptures,

still there after centuries, and having models dressed in togas or not at all, made me feel that nothing had ever changed. I became part of history, understanding what an important part religion has played in art and how difficult it has been for artists who want to depict humans as God made them, innocent and timeless, without clothes. And I understood how the benefactors of art often tried to control the work with artificial and temporary mores. The continuing struggle between the artist and the patron.

During that year, 1990, I was constantly aware of the struggle happening with the NEA, Jesse Helms, and art censorship.

The next year I knew that I needed to return to Italy because there was so much more to learn about life and sculpture, and I needed to return to fill out my photo series with pictures of children depicting angels.

I excitedly showed my photos to the *padrone* of the *laboratorio* where I had worked the previous year. He told me that he was awed by their beauty. Three hours later, however, he delivered a message saying that I could never show these works in Italy because he felt his family would misinterpret the use of nudes with religious sculptures (most of them nude themselves).

I was shocked and discouraged but after a time found another place to sculpt and continue my photo series concentrating on photographing children as angels. I was fortunate to find Yvonne, the beautiful and talented daughter of the sculptor who had won the coveted Prix de Rome for sculpture in 1991. I decided to photograph her in her father's studio with the torso he had made of her. It was a beautiful shoot. Yvonne was a natural and the light, exquisite.

When, after returning to America, I showed the results of that glorious day to a friend, she warned me that shooting photos of a nude child could get me into trouble with the FBI. I laughed and said she must be joking, but she sent me an article about a number of photographers who had been persecuted for this.

At first I decided not to show the photos, though I felt strongly that they were reflections of a beautiful spirit. I have a great fear of contention, but decided

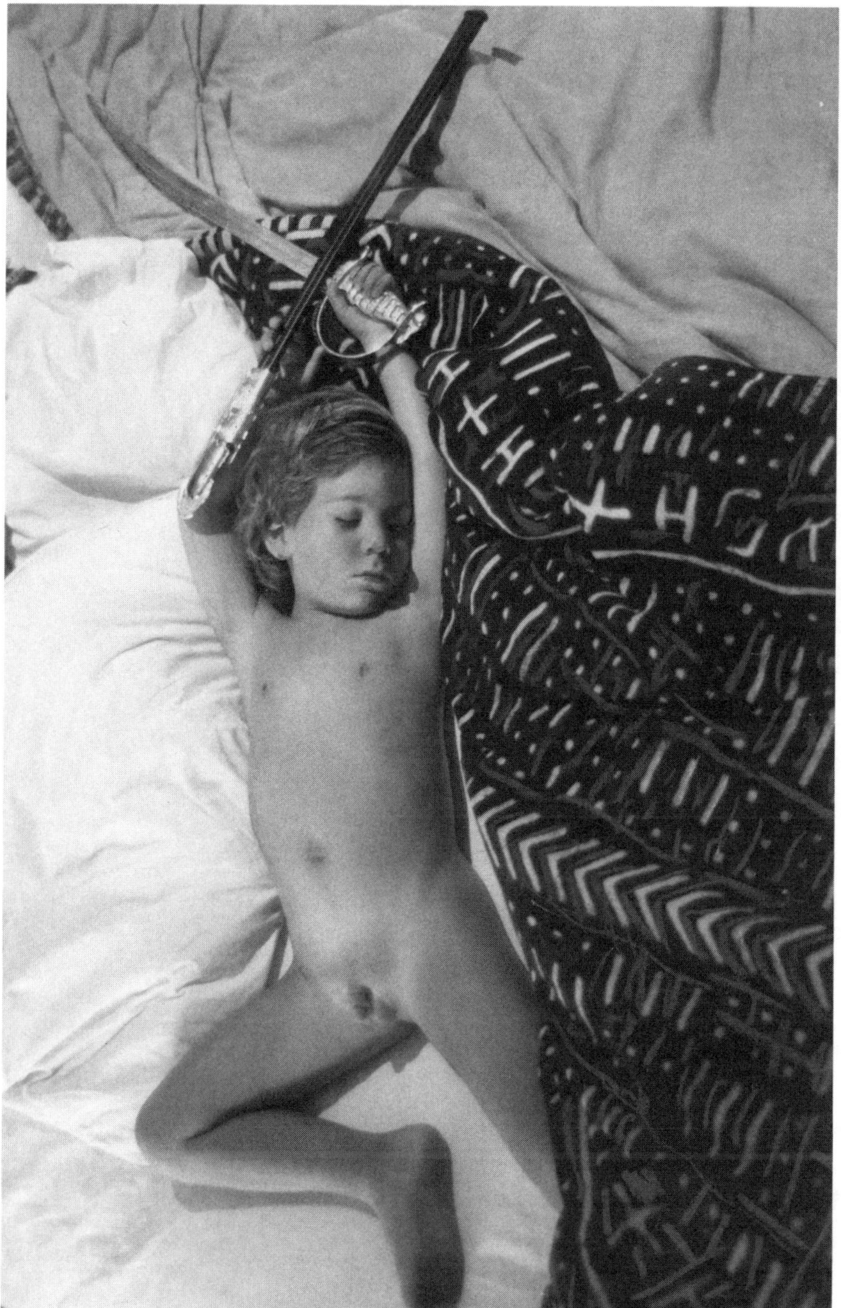

to make my altarpiece anyway. Soon I realized that my series had taken on a political tone. I juxtaposed the nude little boy, symbol of the city of Brussels, with my nude little girl; her face and body alight with all the beauty and spirituality of a religious painting. Here was my answer to Jesse Helms.

The assemblages started taking on names like "Innocence" and "Judgement." I wondered how anything as perfect and pure as the unadorned body of a child, or anybody, depicted by an artist could speak of anything but the wonder of God.

I present these works with the confidence that their beauty and purity will transcend and prevail in the eyes of the beholder.

The Happiest Place on Earth

Sallie Tisdale

I'm just back from my third trip to Disneyland. I visited for the first time at thirteen, courtesy of a grandmother. From that weekend I remember little more than descending into Monsanto's "Adventures in Inner Space" ride, and glancing up to find a giant eye staring at me through a telescope. I rode that ride again and again. "Inner Space" was subsumed into the new and recurring futures of Tomorrowland, and I vanished into adolescence. Except for a single day twelve years ago, I never returned, yet Disneyland always has a familiar, avuncular feel. Disneyland seems obvious, yes, but more than that, inevitable.

Recently I had a windfall, and I looked at my nine-year-old daughter who has a poster of Mickey Mouse on her bedroom door, and I made secret plans. I told her only a few days before we left, a few days to pack and anticipate the details and call Grandma to exclaim about it with a certain wild silliness. Then we flew to Los Angeles, rented a car, drove across town to the hotel, and took the hotel shuttle to Disneyland all in a few hours on a hot Friday in August. The hotel, which I'd picked out of a Column A-B-or-C list at the travel agent, was nearly new, one of many look-alike mountains of rooms thrown up by investors in the crowded, noisy blocks around Disneyland. The wallpaper was beginning to peel, rugs bunched up in the corners. The shower was broken, a light bulb burned out, the door to the balcony stuck shut. Room service plates lay outside a half-dozen doors in the long, empty corridor, the sticky yellow cheese of leftover nachos drying to a rubbery sheen. But from our big corner windows we could see the rumpled gray Matterhorn, and the shuttle waited below.

Every day, beginning around seven o'clock in the morning, cars trickle into the Disneyland parking lot, which is bigger than Disneyland itself. Only in the United States of America is there, could there ever be, a parking lot as big as Disneyland's under a sky as bright and dirty as the sky in Los Angeles. (Excuse me, A*naheim*, as my friends in Los Angeles are quick to remind me.) The streams of cars give way to parking lot shuttles for people who don't want to walk from their cars to the gates, pass the hotel shuttles, and become streams of people, on foot, in strollers, in wheelchairs, small creeks of people converging into rivulets and then rivers, all heading toward the spillway of the narrow gates, where they pile up like a torrent of white water and shove themselves through. We left the shuttle, entered the stream, squeezed through the gates. Coming and going, the signs call Disneyland "The Happiest Place on Earth." And there, right there, right inside, is Winnie the Pooh larger than life, bending clumsily down to pat a child, his Pooh grin never wavering. The thing that works about Disneyland is that it works. We submit. We're glad to be here.

I had bought the trip as a Disney Package, airfare and rental car and hotel and Disney Passports all rolled into one big credit-card charge. Part of the package is something called the Magic Morning, an outdoor breakfast in Disneyland early in the morning, before the park officially opens, attended by a half-dozen characters.

The characters appear without warning, all over the park, cartoon characters come to life, who dash or pad or stomp or dance around depending on their species, and never speak lest the illusion be shattered. Whenever they appear, they draw families with strollers and diaper bags and camcorders, happy kids, and sometimes shy, tearful, frightened kids pressed forward by eager parents. Captain Hook, who stands several inches taller than me and whose hat casts long shadows around him, is greeted by a respectful distance wherever he goes. Snow White, petite, slender, smiling, is happily stroked by toddlers. My nine-year-old, cheerfully growing up as slowly as she can, still believes in Santa Claus and only this summer learned about the Tooth Fairy. She is frightened by clowns. Does she know? I wondered, each time she held her autograph book up to a silent mask. Should I tell her? That morning, at the breakfast, we saw Aladdin, the Genie, Snow White, Eeyore, Pluto, and Tigger. "Tigger!" she screamed, and raced for a hug, smiled for the camera, asked for an autograph. Late that day, she said, "I bet they get hot in those costumes."

As far as I was concerned, the point of Magic Morning wasn't the characters, or the sticky, sweet breakfast, but the park's emptiness. Perhaps a few hundred people shared Tomorrowland and the Matterhorn with us at 7:30 on a crystalline, rosy morning, and they all but disappeared in the silent open spaces. The bustling, noisy herd of the day before was gone as though it had never been. But the emptiness was strange, more dreamy than the rides themselves, and disconcerting.

There is a fine psychology built into Disneyland's long lines, which are well-hidden and bend continually back upon themselves and around corners and through doorways. You have no idea, really, how long a line is until you are unavoidably part of it; the gasp of understanding when you finally see what a 45-minute wait with a child means is held back until you can't change your mind. "If you aren't the sort of person willing to invest an hour of agony for two minutes of joy," says my Disneyland guide, "you probably shouldn't have had children in the first place."

More importantly, the waiting draws you slowly down into each ride's particular shifting world, working bit by bit on one's natural disbelief. Each major ride and each "land" has its own employee costumes and myriad other cues transcribing the borders of the imagined world; each creates, with varying degrees of success, a conditioned response to sights barely seen and sounds barely heard, subtly and casually dropped into the background as though they had no importance, no effect. There is first the willingness to accede to fantasy, and then, without warning, the body's own unwilled and astonishing ability to suspend its own knowledge of reality. So the foyer of Star Tours, an intergalactic travel agency, is rather dull and as bland as a Greyhound bus depot, and the slow descent into Space Mountain takes you into a coolly decorated, impersonal space station designed for maximum bureaucratic efficiency on a cosmic scale. The Matterhorn has a buoyant Alpine bouquet, and you are handled by strapping young Nordic men in lederhosen, and Thunder Mountain, a Wild West roller-coaster, feels hot, arid, and lawless. Splash Mountain is all Brer Rabbit and Zippity-Doo-Dah, and its lines curl slowly along with the tranquil repose of Valium.

On Magic Morning, there were no lines anywhere. We climbed over the fence to leap on the Matterhorn, jogged gleefully up into Star Tours without pausing to listen to C3PO's complaints, and sat in an empty shuttle for our trip. The assembly-line shiver, the sense of being part of some enormous piece of carefully-timed machinery, was gone. My daughter talked me into Space Mountain. One enters first by climbing, up moving sidewalks and then ramps, and then far down a switchback walkway. The ride slowly pulls you up into darkness and then throws you brutally into space like a slingshot. One feels obligated to scream. We screamed with vigor, alone in our car, after two minutes slid into the space station, where no one was waiting. We had only to stay seated a moment to ride again, and again.

When Magic Morning ended and the entire park was about to open for real at 8 AM, we stood with about 50 other Disney Package customers at the edge between Tomorrowland and Main Street, waiting for the security guard's signal. When he looked at his watch and waved us on it was like a Mother's Day stroller dash, the beginning, for many families, of a long day force-feeding high-stimulation fun to small children who preferred to linger at the fountains and watch pigeons, but would not be allowed to do so. Their parents were too willing to be rude on behalf of them, too hungry to see and do, photograph and experience, to fill up, to fill out.

By the afternoon I couldn't stand the place any longer. The crowds are amazing, enormous, they're Hong Kong at rush hour, Tokyo subways, a pan-Manhattan Labor Day sale. Families and camp groups come dressed the same way, moving like schools of fish through the churning rivers of people; Junior and Grandpa and all the cousins dressed in bright green t-shirts and red shorts for easy spotting in the throng. On a busy day, when more than 15,000 cars fill the parking lot and one hotel shuttle after the other disgorges its passengers every half-hour on the hour, and the monorail fills up at the enormous Disneyland Hotel with more guests for the park again and again, there may be fifty or sixty thousand people inside at the same time. And they're all in line, or rushing to the end of one.

Then, near the "60-minute-wait from here" sign, I watched a Space Mountain employee patiently try to explain to a large family why the ride has a height requirement, why the very tiny girl with bows in her hair, holding Daddy's hand and standing mutely near the moving sidewalk, could not be allowed to go on the scariest ride in the park. They wanted to argue. I wanted to go. So we tramped back to Main Street, through the gates to get our invisible, indelible hand stamps, back through the parking lot to wait for the shuttle, back to the empty hotel hallways, the water stained wallpaper, the silent view of the shadeless parking lot crawling with cars.

My friend Harry, who lives in Beverly Hills, refused to come see me in Anaheim. He never goes to Anaheim, he tells me, loftily. And I won't go to him. I'm exhausted, beaten into submission, dozing by the pool, gathering strength for another onslaught. My daughter seems as happy to bob in the pale blue water as she was to ride Space Mountain. "No one ever comes here to go to Disneyland and does *anything* else," he tells me, but he's wrong. Our package included One Other Attraction, we could have gone to Knott's Berry Farm or Universal Studios, and lots of people are doing that around us, packing up the kids into the rental car and driving all over hell and back for another parking lot, more long lines, big crowds, more sensation. We used ours for a third day in Disneyland.

When Disneyland opened in 1955 a complicated intellectual debate began — about Disneyland as a work of art, as a cultural artifact, a piece of architecture, a symbol of capitalism. It was, above all, taken seriously. The debate seemed to end, without conclusion, decades ago, and now Disneyland is treated as a lark. (Except, that is, as a market force, where Disneyland is taken very seriously indeed.) Most people I know treat a trip to Disneyland as an indulgence just for the kids, a kind of mental slumming. Disneyland is low-class fun, *lower-class* no matter what it costs. Disneyland is *common*. One definition of common, of course, is whatever satisfies the masses. But in fact Disneyland is uncommon to a fault, it's unique, unrepeatable. The park and everything in it is well made, never tawdry or thin in any way; its textures are always complex and layered. And Disneyland is awfully good at what it does.

Everywhere, an incredible attention to detail. Everything unsightly, disturbing, or mindful of ordinary life is hidden from sight. Thirty tons of trash are collected every *day* in Disneyland, twelve million pounds a year, the detritus of four million hamburgers and more than a million gallons of soda pop, and rarely is there a single straw wrapper on the ground, never does a trash can overflow or a distant glimpse of a garbage truck mar the view. It has always been thus, always a miracle of anal-retentive inspection, compulsive control, unceasing surveillance. The park was built on the bones of orange groves in a year and a day by workers using only hand tools, workers who are always smiling in the photographs. In fact, they went on strike several times during that year, the park wasn't actually finished when it opened, and the opening day was an unmitigated disaster. But in the Disney tradition, people have forgotten all that now.

The intense orderliness of Disneyland, its extremes of cleanliness and unflagging courtesy, its Teutonic precision and appalling vision, and especially the way it deliberately shuts out the niggling problems of reality and gives us an illusion of goodness are all deliberate. Walt Disney was a hard-drinking, pill-popping, anti-union, Communist-baiting, bad-tempered man, an obsessive, depressive, control freak. He gave names to the House Un-American Activities Committee and proudly informed for the FBI. Disney was stingy, mildly anti-Semitic, and feared death so badly he investigated cryonics. But Disney was never cynical. He was amazingly uncynical, in fact. Disneyland is the world he wanted to live in, and as soon as he could build it, he did.

Disney's world is one of impulse without risk, childish spontaneity devoid of danger. All is cued and manipulated, telegraphed and choreographed, manufactured, manicured. Disneyland offers freedom from decision in the guise of endless choice, freedom from confusion, from having to do anything we don't want to do. (Except wait in line, which makes the fun more virtuous.) Even the grand fireworks are introduced over the park-wide public-address system by an unseen Big Brother with a primetime commercial voice, soothing and boosterish, their explosions accompanied by patriotic music to be sure we all understand the point. Disneyland is an exceptionally smart place, a conception of wide-ranging intelligence which allows visitors to be as stupid as they could possibly be and still breathe.

And more. Disneyland is a dream that flitters with genius and then turns into the repeating shrieks of nightmare without warning. (One friend of mine compares it to a particularly bad episode of "The Prisoner.") In every Disney film there's a moment when the cheerful music turns sour or threatening, when the Sorcerer's Apprentice realizes he can't stop the water coming, when Dumbo's mother screams in grief, chained in the dark. In every film the giggles of psilocybin eventually give way to the mania of speed. Disneyland is Pleasure Island from *Pinocchio*, the island of endless fun that ruins you if you stay a moment too long. As Richard Shickel wrote, it's a dream without any of the dark, dangerous elements that are the essential characteristics of real dreams. There is no incongruity, no unpredictability. No sex, no violence, except the childish sex of an Animatronic pirate and the bloodless violence of cartoons. As a dream, Disneyland isn't much good for therapy. It's more a daydream than anything else, closer to Marie Antoinette than Carl Jung.

    I can't imagine working here, spending every day in this amalgam of the excruciating and the sublime. After we watched the 3-D Michael Jackson movie, *Captain* EO, the young man in charge said to the crowd, "Thank you for coming," and "Have a nice day," and then murmured into the microphone, "I'*m* going to stay and see the show again. And again and again and again." I listened to "It's a Small World" for 15 minutes while waiting in line and tried to imagine listening to it on tinkly speakers *all day long*. We were caught in the Electrical Parade mob and literally couldn't get out, at one point I couldn't even stand up from where I'd sat down, there was no room and no one would give an inch, and I was underneath one of the enormous speakers hanging discretely from a tree, blaring the tinny parade music over and over, and I tried to imagine being Mickey Mouse on the lead float, dancing and smiling and dancing to that music until one day I just snapped and pulled an automatic weapon out of Mickey's pocket and went boom. Bye-bye Donald Duck. Bye-bye Pooh.

I'm seduced again. I buy iced tea on a sunny morning and sit on an ironwork bench in the Main Street Square, and the sudden, intense pleasure I feel isn't just because Main Street is, literally, a scale model; it's not just that the bricks and lamps and shingles are all 5/8 normal size and the second story doors and windows are deliberately foreshortened that gives me a powerful sense of peace. There is something curiously, fundamentally, safe here. There is a woman on the bench opposite me, slowly rocking a stroller with her foot. Here comes the little fire engine, right on time. Here is the ice cream parlor, the magic shop, the candy store. There is Goofy in the distance, nodding and smiling and nodding and smiling. That night, at twilight, as we swung slowly in the tram above the park, a great splash of crows swooped into the tall eucalyptus trees around us, across a clear, abalone sky, and I couldn't imagine wanting to be anywhere else.

I'm seduced, too, by the genuine pleasure around me, the cheerful diversity of all I see. I explain how to use the pay-token lockers to a Mexican family who speak only Spanish. We ride the lovely Whirling Teacups with a Japanese nuclear family and a trio of green-haired tattooed teenagers all having the same wonderful time spinning in the morning light. I see time and again how many pubescent girls ride the Storybook Land boats without a shred of wistfulness. I see a woman in a Christian Fellowship t-shirt standing next to a handsome young man in a "Nobody Knows I'm a Lesbian" t-shirt. I see two little old ladies flying into the Peter Pan ride alone; that night two little old men elbow me out of the way for seats at the parade. Time and again, I hear conversations around me in the long lines — reminiscences of Disneyland ten, twenty, thirty years ago, sparkling images carried on into adulthood and cherished always, to be passed to one's own children later, today, now.

Over the years, a tradition of private graduation and prom night parties has developed at Disneyland. What could be safer for teenagers wanting a good time? Now, I'm told, any group can rent the park in its off-hours. "*Any* group?" I ask, disbelieving, still digesting Walt Disney's peculiar political beliefs. "I can't think who we'd turn away," I'm told, and I don't press the matter with suggestions. So Disneyland hosts Scout troop celebrations and church parties and business outings. Twenty years ago my friend Nancy got herself kicked out of Disneyland for dancing with a girl, but now there's an unofficial Gay and Lesbian Night in the park every year.

Disneyland is separate-but-equal opportunity, it's parallelism, a globe along which the lines of latitude never meet. Disneyland is a just world, an evenhanded declaration that we are all the same, except that we're different, and isn't difference wonderful? Wonderful in this democratic utopia of happy segregation. While Mickey Mouse's House is filled with books and games and machinery, Minnie Mouse's House next door is filled only with the paraphernalia of beauty and her lists of things to do for Mickey Mouse. In the Main Street Electrical Parade, which happens two times every evening, all the women are blondes, all of them, dozens of them, with the unavoidable exception of Snow White and the perhaps not conscious redheadedness of Cinderella's Wicked Stepsisters.

"It's A Small World," supposedly the quintessential celebration of diversity, has virtually no Indians, only a cheerful little maiden next to a cheerful little cowboy. So we went to the ride's own official toy store next door, and found that it has no "It's A Small World" dolls. The store, like the ride, is "sponsored" by Mattel, as though Disneyland were some church-run charity needing corporate largesse, and sells only Disney character dolls, a few other action figures, and Barbies. Lots of Barbies, Jamaican Barbie and Eskimo Barbie and Japanese Barbie, lined up on the shelf next to Army Barbie and Army Ken.

Only employees with vaguely Persian features work at Aladdin's care, only pert white teenage girls work at Storybook Land. There is never a black Cinderella and never a blonde Princess Jasmine. The fact that small children who love these characters wouldn't care if Cinderella was black isn't important. Neither is the fact that the enduring characters like Mickey Mouse aren't even human. These carefully drawn dividing lines are part of the precision, the vision, the idea — the ideal.

As I hang in an open car on a slim cable above the park, as the Matterhorn bobsled begins its clackety climb, as we shoot down into the dark humidity of the Pirates of the Caribbean, I imagine disaster. I see its possibility in every bolt and cotter pin. There is regular disaster planning, but rarely any kind of disaster here, and those are small, individual, human-sized ones. Occasional heart attacks whisked quickly away by ambulance, purse-snatchings, epileptic fits, sprained ankles. There have been only a few well-publicized deaths, like that of a woman who stood up on the Matterhorn and fell. In the mid-1980s an employee took a shortcut through the

Carousel of Progress and, in a monumentally ironic moment, was crushed by the machinery like Charlie Chaplin in the assembly line. Murders, suicides, fires seem not to exist inside the walls. Even Los Angeles' almost-yearly earthquakes have never damaged Disneyland. Now and then a ride stalls. When Splash Mountain first opened it broke down at least once a week, requiring the smiling, cheerful employees to walk passengers out through the emergency exits, hidden inside giant bumblebee hives and behind fat talking bears.

If Los Angeles is anarchy, then Disneyland is fascism. And like Los Angeles, Disneyland seems an impossible, post-apocalyptic place at times. Suddenly I see the enormous potential for political action here. But again, hardly any such thing ever happens. The most memorable event was in 1970, when a band of Yippies took over Tom Sawyer Island and raised the Communist flag over the fort. As we ride through the Small World ("It's a small world, *after all! It's a small* world, *after* all!") I imagine Native Americans climbing out of the boats to stand in defiance inside the mechanical doll displays. ("It's a world of laughter, a world of tears!") I imagine drag queens lining up with the auctioned women in Pirates of the Caribbean, Black Panthers joining the headhunters on the Jungle Cruise. I have visions of sabotage, terrorism, the unspeakable heresies possible here. I imagine vandalizing Tinkerbell's harness. Something truly big and daring. Yet the most dramatic thing I saw was a series of "Out of Order" signs taped to trees. Finally, I call the Disneyland publicity department and ask about terrorism. The P.R. man I talk to seems surprised at the idea. "That's not why people come to Disneyland," he says.

✧

And then I find myself sliding effortlessly, and in fact involuntarily, unwillingly, back into bliss, riding the steam train around the park. I AM breathless at the elaborate fireworks. I get misty-eyed listening to a robot of Abe Lincoln talk about healing. We eat lunch at the Blue Bayou, a pseudo-Cajun restaurant perched inside the Pirates of the Caribbean, under a moonlit, starry New Orleans sky, cooled by light breezes, listening to the locusts. My daughter meets Mickey Mouse for the first time.

Outside the park is a messy, blurred world. Inside one finds only clear boundaries and distinct expectations. This vision, this hope, that such a world as this could be is promulgated so well and so deeply that for moments — sterling, distinct moments, Magic Moments — our very lives seem safe and free. A true generosity fills the heart, we are joined in a community without threat. We wait our turn. We smile at the child who waits restlessly beside us.

My brother remembers, with a surprising intensity, his first visit to Disneyland at the age of twelve. He had all the world in his hands that day, and he spent all its hours on Tom Sawyer Island, chasing other whooping, wild twelve-year-olds through a fantasy of pure boyhood. When he told me this, I thought about how different twelve-year-olds are these days. But perhaps, for a time on Tom Sawyer Island, even now they're all the same.

The Root of the Game

Juan Armando Epple
Translated by Ken Inness

Let's you be the mom and me be the dad.

And you cook and send the children off to school, and check on them in the afternoons to make sure they do their homework, and tell them off. And me I work in the factory and don't come home until it's practically night and ask Did the kids eat yet? And you answer Yes but you sent them to bed because they were being brats, they stole some sugar cubes, they ripped their pants, they broke one of the neighbor's windows, that sort of thing. And since I put bread on the table I say real loud so everyone can hear That's too bad, since I was going to give them a little something to spend but now I'll have to hold on to it and see if they can straighten up tomorrow, and then I'll give it to them anyway so they can buy ice cream and candy, or maybe I won't. But for all I know the kids will act just fine they next day, and so before they leave for school I give them what I promised, so they can have something in their pockets just like grown-ups. And then I shake their heads around with this huge hand of mine and I tell them These kids are going to work harder than their folks, and I'll bet they even go places, and then you'll get mad because I muss up their hair and 'cause it's getting late, and you'll say There you go, spoiling them again, but I'll just smile.

This shoe box can be the TV and you can turn it on every morning and watch "Days of Our Lives" and then you just sit for a spell and forget all about the bread burning in the oven.

Let's have these be the plates and these be the spoons. And we can bring a little dirt from the garden, but not the sawdust because Dad gets mad, since it's for that heater he made out of the barrel where we used to hide when he came in from work whistling, and screamed like he was scared when we came out with our guns and made him stick 'em up. And we'll need the billfold for shopping, since Mom likes to take it along because it's white and she says it goes good with her Sunday shoes, and you like it because it matches your dress.

And then let's have you go to the market on Saturdays and bring back vegetables, these grass clippings, and fruit. I'm going to look for an apple because now nobody will care, and we'll cut it up into little pieces and they can be whole apples. And then you can come back and we'll be here playing and enjoying ourselves, but you go in the house and forget to check our homework, you leave the billfold in the recliner and look toward the kitchen and say This ain't living, and then we go hide in the oil drum hoping that Dad comes back whistling real loud because tomorrow is Sunday and so he's gonna want me to look for his horseshoes, and I wipe them with a cloth until they're really clean, now it doesn't really matter anymore if I shine them with my shirt sleeve, and he says to me Let's rack up some points before lunch, kiddo.

And these stones can be the horseshoes, but it's better if I go look for the real ones, even if it isn't Sunday.

And I can also be the photographer who goes door to door, since it's kind of sort of boring just playing horseshoes by myself while you prepare the mud.

Give me a can since you aren't going to use all of them for making supper. Let's make a little hole here, and it'll be the camera.

Then I'll come up to you and say Ma'am, I represent Photo-Art Incorporated and I am now offering my services to private households. We do color photography, pastel colorizations…was it 'pattel'?, okay, we can do a fine group portrait, it doesn't matter if everybody isn't home right now because we have a patented process by which we can copy the photos given to us by our customers, and then we put them all together in one picture, in color. Like a puzzle, get it? And let's say you don't want it at first but then you decide you do, and you show me the album we had on the dresser and I ask Which is the most recent photo of your husband?

Let's say I keep coming with my camera and make friends with the children because I bring them candy and later on I give them money so they can go off and buy things. And you'll be watching through the window waiting for me, and now you'll laugh more often because you'd like to take that color portrait I'm working on and put it in the dining room, and it doesn't matter if it takes a while because you know it's a lot of work, and each time I come I tell you nice things about art, funny things, and with practically none of you really seeing how you want me to come to the house in the morning and stay a while, and I'll help myself to some little thing you're cooking up, and when I leave I remind the children that the picture is a secret and that Dad shouldn't know anything until it's ready. But then we end up not talking about the picture anymore because what really matters to us is that the photographer man sends us off to buy things like cigarettes and sodas, and we take off running even though it's a long way, because we get to keep the change.

In the meantime you can clean up or fix supper and me I'll put on this wool cap or the hard-hat that's in the tool shed and let's have me be Dad and I come home all upset because they fired me from the factory just before the strike, even though I'm on the union committee, and I walk on in without even getting scared when we tell him to stick 'em up, and I come through the kitchen door and bump into the photographer and I punch him out because he still hasn't done the picture like we told him to. And there'll be a big fight, pow, bam, and the chairs get knocked over and the vase gets broken and you scream, all scared, but I win and the photographer runs off and forgets his jacket, but not his camera.

And then I get mad at you too, and you shake

all over and your hair will be a mess and I'll jerk you out of the room where you're cleaning up and I'll shove you real hard against the cupboard and you scream and fall down crying, and bit by bit you'll stop sobbing and you'll just lay there on the floor like you're sleeping when we go in to see what is the matter.

And then let's have me stand there next to you, thinking and being serious, but I pick up the apples that fell during the fight and put them back in their place.

And then I whisper something, with my lips pulled tight so the children don't hear, like I'm praying.

And then let's say the police arrive, the ones in green fatigues, and come in with the photographer 'cause he has been working for the military government too and they ask me questions, but not us kids.

And they take you away very carefully so as not to wake you up, because you're so sick, and maybe you won't get around to seeing the portrait, and they take you to the hospital in the ambulance, and this whistle can be the siren, but don't cry anymore because we're not going to fight ever, okay? Go ahead, blow on it and make that long sound like you know how to do, and let's have me ask the police sergeant if they'll at least let me take a blanket, and I won't see the photographer, who comes in and takes one because I'm staring out the window and I wipe away my sweat or my tears with my sleeve, like kids do, before those men take me away in their truck, and we the children have to stay in the patio by ourselves, playing all day.

La Raiz del Juego

Juan Armando Epple

Que tú seas la mamá y yo el papá.

Tú que hagas la comida y mandes los niños a la Escuela, y que les revises si hacen las tareas en la tarde y les tengas que tirar las orejas. Y yo que salga a trabajar a la fábrica y vuelva casi de noche, y diga ¿los niños ya comieron? y tu contestas que sí pero que los mandaste a la cama porque hicieron barbaridades, se robaron unos terrones de azúcar, se rompieron el pantalón, le quebraron un vidrio de la ventana al vecino, cosas así. Y yo que te entregue la plata para la casa, para pagar las cuentas del almacén, y diga fuerte, para que todos escuchen: que lástima, porque les tenía un premio a los ninos pero voy a tener que guardarme estas moneditas en mi bolsillo a ver si mañana se portan mejor, y entonces se las doy para que compren helados o dulces, o si no no. Pero que yo sepa ya que al otro día los niños se van a portar bien, y por eso antes de que salgan para la Escuela que les entregue el premio que les prometí, para que tengan para el bolsillo como las personas grandes. Que les sacuda la cabeza con esta mano grandota y les diga: estos cabros van a salir más aplicados que los papás, y apuesto a que van a llegar más lejos, y tú que te enojes porque los despeino y se hace tarde y digas: ya me los estás malcriando otra vez, pero que yo sonría.

Que esta caja de zapatos sea una radio y que tú la pongas todas las mañanas en la Baquedano para escucha Calvario de Amor, y te quedes sentada un rato en la cocina, olvidando el pan que se está quemando en el horno.

Que estos sean los platos y estas las cucharas. Para hacer el pan traemos un poco de tierra del jardin, pero el aserrín no porque el papá se enoja, es para ese calentador que hizo con el tambor donde nos escondíamos cuando llegaba del trabajo silbando, y gritaba como asustándose cuando salíamos con los fusiles para tomarlo manos arriba. La cartera sí porque sirve para ir a las compras, y a la mamá le gusta llevarla porque es blanca y dice que le hace juego con los zapatos del domingo, y a tí que te haga Juego con el vestido.

Tú que vayas a comprar a la feria del sábado y traigas las verduras, este pastito, y las frutas. Voy a buscar una manzana porque ahora nadie va a reclamar y la cortamos en pedacitos y esos que sean manzanas enteras. Entonces que vuelvas y nosotros que estemos contentos jugando, pero tú entras en la casa y te olvidas revisarnos las tareas, dejas la cartera en el sillón y miras hacia la cocina diciendo: esto no es vida, y nosotros que vayamos a escondernos en el tarro esperando que venga mi papá silbando más fuerte porque al otro dia es domingo y entonces me va a pedir que le busque sus tejos, yo se los limpio hasta sacarle brillo con el gangocho, no importaque ahora los limpe con la manga de la camisa, y que me diga: vamos a probar puntería antes del almuerzo, cabrito.

Que estas piedras sean los tejos, pero mejor voy a buscar los tejos de verdad, aunque no sea domingo.

Y también que sea el fotógrafo que pasa por las casas, porque es medio aburrido que que me esté jugando sólo a los tejos, mientras amasas ese barro.

Dame un tarro, que no los vas a usar todos para hacer la cornida. Le hacemos un hoyito aquí y que sea la máquina de sacar fotos.

Yo que venga entonces con mi máquina de sacar fotos y te diga: señora, soy representante de Foto-Arte y estoy ofreciendo mis servicios a domicilio. Hacemos fotos en clores, en pastel...¿era en panel?, bueno, podemos hacer un lindo grupo familiar, no importa que no estén todos en la casa en este momento, porque tenemos una patente esclusiva donde podemos copiar las fotos que nos dan nuestros clientes y después se las entregamos juntas en un cuadro, y en colores. Como un rompecabezas, ¿sabe? Y tú que primero no quieras pero después si, y que me muestres el áibum que teníamos en la alacena y yo te pregunte; ¿cuál es la foto más reciente de su marido?

Yo que pase otras veces con mi máquina y me haga amigo de los niños, porque les traigo dulce y más adelante les doy plata para que vayan a comprar. Y tú que me mires a veces por la ventana viendo si me acordé de pasar a verlos, y ahora te rías más porque te gustaría poner en el comedor ese cuadro en colores que estoy haciendo y no importa que se demore porque sabes que es un trabajo difícil, y yo cada vez te doy explicaciones muy bonitas sobre el arte, muy graciosas, y casi sin darse cuenta ustedes van deseando que yo llegue en la mañana a la casa y me quede largo rato conversando, me sirva alguna cosita que tú estás preparando y cuando me vaya les recuerde a los niños que el cuadro es un secreto y que el papá no debe saber nada hasta que esté terminado. Aunque al final ya no hablemos casi del cuadro, porque a nosotros nos interesa más que el señor fotógrafo nos encargue que vayamos a comprar algo, cigarrillos, bebidas, para salir corriendo, aunque sea lejos, porque podemos recortarnos algo del vuelto.

Tú mientras tanto que hagas el aseo o la cornida y yo me Bongo este gorro de lana o el casco de trabajo que está en la pieza de las herramientas y soy el papá, y que venga preocupado porque me echaron de la fábrica justo antes de la huelga, aunque estoy en la directiva, y que Base sin querer asustarme cuando lo tomamos manos arriba y entre Bor la puerta de la cocina, y que encuentre al fotógrafo y entonces le pegue porque todavía no nos ha traído el cuadro que mandamos a hacer. Que haya una pelea bien grande, paf, pum, que se caigan las sillas y se quiebre el jarrón de las flores y tú que grites asustada pero yo gano, y el fotógrafo que salga corriendo y se olvide de su chaqueta, pero no de su máquina.

Entonces que yo me enoje también contigo,

que estás temblando y toda despeinada. Que te saque del dormitorio donde has estado haciendo las piezas y te de un empujón fuerte, te golpees la cabeza contra la alacena y grites y después caigas llorando cada vez más despacito, hasta que te quedes acurrucadita allí en el piso, como si estuvieras durmiendo cuando entramos a ver qué pasó.

Yo que me quede parado a tu lado, pensando, y que esté cada vez más serio y más triste, pero que recoja las manzanas que se han caído con la pelea y las ponga en su lugar.

Y luego que diga unos garabatos despacito, con los labios apretados para que no oigan los niños, como si estuviera rezando.

Y entonces que vengan los policías, vestidos de militares, y entren con el fotógrafo porque también les hacia fotos a ellos, y que le hagan preguntas a mi papá pero a nosotros no.

Que a ti te tomen entonces con cuidado para no despertarte, porque te has quedado muy enferma y quizás ya cuándo verás ese retrato, y que te lleven en la ambulancia al Hospital y que este pito sea la sirena, pero tú ahora no llores porque nosotros no vamos a pelearnos nunca, ¿quieres?, anda, tócalo tú con ese sonido largo que sabes sacarle, y yo que le pida al jefe de los policías que me dejen llevar por lo menos una manta, y no vea al fotógrafo que entra a la pieza y saca una frazada porque me pongo a mirar por la ventana y me limpio el sudor o las lágrimas con la manga, como hacen los niños, antes de que me lleven esos hombres en su camión y nosotros nos tengamos que quedar solos en el patio, jugando todo el día.

A Wing and a Prayer

Virginia Euwer Wolff

A giant storm came blowing down on Trout Creek Ridge in the autumn of 1944, after the apple and pear harvests were over. The wind broke fruit trees in half, it pulled doors off garages, it knocked ladders into the sides of pickups, it turned over the washbench on our back porch, it tossed buckets all the way across the lawn, and it woke everybody in the night. Our cow was so frightened her milk didn't come right for two days.

The storm made all the ice cream in McHenry's Store melt because they had electricity there, and when the storm came it blew a Douglas fir tree down on top of the electric wires between the school and the store. There was no electricity anywhere for a long time. Not in the school, not in the store, not in the church. So all the ice cream melted and the McHenrys got to eat it all up like soup. Jerry McHenry was in first grade with me and he was fat at his stomach and on his hands.

The electric poles leaned all the way to the ground like Tinkertoys, and the tree lay there with the electric wires tangled. No cars could go through town and everybody had the day off for a while. Jerry McHenry's grandfather, old J.T. McHenry, limped out on the store porch and looked at the mess all over the road out front and shook his wrinkly head back and forth. "Lord

Mercy," he said. Young McHenrys were fat but they got skinny with hairy arms when they got old. J.T. McHenry was so old he had been in the first war, the one where soldiers went to France. He had a crooked leg from that war.

A photograph of old J.T. McHenry hung on the wall in the back part of the store where he and Jerry McHenry's father had their desks. In the picture he was a hero in that other war. Old J.T. McHenry went back there, and he sent Jerry McHenry's father around the north road to get my friend Kate's father to come and bring his saw. Kate's father came in his rattly truck and sawed the tree for two days, making the whole town smell woody. I got to watch if I stood exactly by Kate's mother and her baby, because Kate was in my grade. They got to take a truckload of pieces home for their heating stove. The Principal's husband and the janitor stacked wood up high against the back wall of the school for the school furnace, and the McHenry men stacked a big pile against the side of the store. Old J.T. McHenry took the rest of the wood on the store truck over to the church for the furnace there. School started again and they got more ice cream in McHenry's.

At the church they let some poor people from the East Side farms come and get wood to take home. The minister said it in church. "Those without farwood come and take some to warm their homes. You all let your neighbors know, brothers and sisters."

The other fallen tree was the one that crashed down behind the playground at school. It was a Douglas fir too. The boys played War at it, down the hill at the end where the whole roots of the tree had come ripping out of the ground. They shot their sticks from behind the fallen tree, even down in the enormous hole the tree used to be growing out of, and when they fell down they said "Aiiieeeee!" They fell backwards, their legs kicking up. They grabbed their stomachs when they fell, and some of them dropped their sticks, others fell with their sticks still in their hands. Boys were all over the ground by the time recess was finished.

The Principal made a rule that the eighth-grade boys couldn't play at the fallen tree till afternoon recess. Everybody else got to have their turn first. "Eighth graders are mature, they can wait their turn" was the rule.

We began to make a girls' playhouse in the top branches of the tree, where it lay on the ground up the hill near the swings, at recess time on the first day of school after the storm. The smell was the best part of the tree playhouse. The sheltering branches had a prickly bright smell, and when we went back inside to have school again we always smelled like tree. Our hands and our coats.

Ellen had a whole set of doll dishes so she got to be the boss of the playhouse. When we were arranging our places, Shadean looked out through the branches of our kitchen and said to a big boy walking past us, "Who are they being? The boys. Down there."

The big boy said, "War men."

"What kind of war men?" Shadean said.

"The Chaps," he said, and ran down the hill to the War end.

I watched Shadean listening. "The Chaps," she said to me. "That's the Chaps down there," she said. We made our playhouse till the huge bell rang in the tower, and we went in to have arithmetic time. We used crayons in counting, and our team was supposed to count by 2's.

On the way into the school building, at the foot of the big stairs, I heard somebody's teacher yelling at the big boys for getting their clothes all dirty, and I heard some of them saying "Aiiieeeee!" again. They had to go back down the stairs and go to the back of the line.

It was the Chaps and the Nazis and the Allies having the war that made us black out our lights on some nights. If we didn't do the blackouts, we'd get bombed.

The Principal also made a fallen tree rule for girls. The eighth-grade girls could play there at the same time with the little ones, but they had to have their Army Hospital in the middle section of the tree. They weren't supposed to go anywhere near our fir cone room dividers.

The Army Hospital tried to have wounded patients from the War at the end of the fallen tree so they could do their Red Cross bandaging, but the soldiers kept getting up and getting healed. So the eighth-grade girls played Rationing and War Bonds, and they mailed V-

Mail in the branches of the middle section of the tree.

Rationing was because of Pearl Harbor which was a bomb that started the war. The Nazis and the Allies needed so much sugar that we couldn't have it unless we had the red and blue ration stamps. Butter was rationed too. Darrel and Donald in school didn't have a cow, so my mother gave them butter from our cow. They gave us purple jam their mother made because we didn't have any purple.

If we had dimes from home on Mondays, we got to go into the eighth-grade classroom and stand in line to buy War Stamps. If we bought War Stamps, we were helping make parachutes and airplanes and jeeps to win the war. And we could also see the eighth-graders sitting at their desks with their big books. And if we bought War Stamps, we got to lick them and paste them in the War Stamp Books.

We brought in nickels for United China Relief. "$1.00 will provide food, shelter, and medical care for a homeless Chinese child for a month," it said when Mrs. Pelley read it to us. "Could we put our nickels together to make a dollar?" she wanted to know. We thought we could, so we did.

We also had scrap metal. We brought in cans and old pots with holes in them and even pieces of toys that didn't work anymore. Shadean had two baby buggies, so she brought in the bent wheels from the old one. The metal would build a B-19 and other things to win the war. Ellen brought the roof of her merry-go-round that had stopped going around. When Donald brought in the oven door from the stove behind their garage, Mrs. Pelley told him he could be first in line for the most metal brought in on the scales that weighed what we brought. His oven door would make four hand grenades to win the war. Then Donald said he could bring in the whole stove, but Mrs. Pelley said that was too much metal for him to bring to school.

"The war needs the metal but the stove is too much metal?" said Donald, blurting out. "That's crazy. You're crazy."

Mrs. Pelley didn't like the way Donald blurted out, so she sent him marching right to the Principal. "You go marching right to the Principal," she told him, and she put her hand on his back so she could send good behavior through his shirt to the inside of him. She watched him walk across the hall to the Principal where eighth grade was. He came back even late for lunch, and we were already on the lima beans. He got to be first in line for afternoon recess and for coats-on, but that was all.

At recess the boys played Flying Fortress too long and they got in trouble. They had to do all the erasers for the first grade and the second grade and even the third grade. Then they had a Commando fight with the erasers, and they couldn't have War at the deep end of the tree for three straight days. Jerry McHenry had to sweep the whole back part of the store, his father was so mad he misbehaved in school.

We played Shortage in our playhouse. We couldn't have sugar or bacon or steak. Ellen's father had to go to the war, and her mother had to go to the shipyards. So she was moving away and Shadean got to have her place as boss. Ellen forgot to take her doll dish set, and we were going to put it in a package with a letter from the whole class, but we never did. So we had Ellen's plates and cups, even with handles not broken off except one. Little Peggy was in charge of them.

The fallen tree was so big that our house had a high wall, and we had very strong branches to swing on. And with a little fir branch you could sweep the hard dirt floor of the playhouse completely clean and then make the boundaries around the rooms with fir cones. There were some rooms in that playhouse where all of us could have meetings to find out Announcements about the Air Raids. There were rooms where we could hide from the bombs, and rooms where we stored secret sugar so our children wouldn't find it and eat it all up.

When Kate left her doll blanket in the fallen tree playhouse from Friday till Monday and it got all soaked and frozen and covered with mud and pitch and prickers, her father came to school and he yelled.

He yelled, "can't keep your kids under control," and he yelled, "sloppy careless," and he yelled, "get my goat."

73

Mrs. Pelley's face was very surprised and irritated, and she tried to make us not hear him but she couldn't. He yelled and he yelled and Kate had to go home with him, with him pulling her along slanting, she couldn't even stand up straight he was pulling her so hard.

After they went down the big staircase his voice was still high in the room, way up by the window tops, pieces of his loudness sticking to the corners. Mrs. Pelley said we would do art next, even though it was time for reading practice, and we got out the colored paper and scissors and paste, and we made apples and grapes and oranges for the windows.

When we were Scotch-taping our oranges onto the window, looking down into the woods below the playground, Shadean pointed down there and said that tree had a hex on it. "I won't play there anymore my whole life. It's bad luck, it's a hex," she said.

I looked out there to where the woods just began and the tree was lying there from the storm. It was the place where the Chaps fell down "Aiiieeeee!" and where the Flying Fortress bombed all the Nazis, and it was our playhouse for the Shortage and the eighth-grade girls' Army Hospital all in the same place. That tree was longer than a telephone pole.

"Not even play Shortage ever? You mean ever again?" I said.

Shadean shook her head, meaning very much not ever again.

We would be in first grade for a long time, and then we had the whole second grade to go to, and then third where they got to have Arithmetic Baseball and the Hat Contest. Still, after years and years, we would be going to this same school, even when we had the Principal for our teacher of eighth grade.

"What will we do then?" I was asking — not even Shadean — not her completely. I was asking our future lives.

"There's a hex there, I won't play there. You can if you want to get hexed," she said.

We made finger designs in the fog our breath made on the cold glass. I couldn't see how every single person playing there could get a hex.

"A hex is more stronger than even a whole school of children," said Shadean.

Mrs. Pelley said, "Girls, girls, put your oranges up and come *on*." We finished taping our oranges to the glass and sat down in our seats.

∿∿∿

Shadean never went back to the fallen tree playhouse. "I'm good to my word," she said, and she got four girls to go with her over to the basement door railing where they made a hideout with branches from mostly alder trees, not any from that fallen Douglas fir. After I got my leg scraped and bleeding on the tree bark from being knocked into it when Little Peggy fell hard from a bomb blast from the Chaps, I played over there at the basement door hideout too. Little Peggy moved Ellen's doll dish set over there, and we took care of our babies there, even when they all got chicken pox. We adopted some homeless Chinese children too, besides our own babies, so it was very crowded.

Kate said she never liked the fallen Douglas fir playhouse anyway.

I thought she liked it. She played ironing there and also Air Raid, and she made beds for the babies. But she promised she hadn't liked it, even back then when we had Shortage there.

Ellen came back to Trout Creek Ridge one day, and she brought her knitting to show us how she could knit and Pearl khaki wool to win the war. Pearl was for the Pearl Harbor bomb. She knitted and Pearled a whole row and back again the opposite way to show us. It was to keep soldiers warm in the war, but it was only like a potholder. "If everybody knitted and Pearled we would win the war," said Ellen. Mrs. Pelley said Ellen was a very good knitter. We gave Ellen back two of her doll dishes that weren't lost yet. She only came back for one half of a day, not even for lunch because her mother had to go back to weld ships.

The rationing with stamps made grownups very upset. The red stamps and the blue ones changed all the time in how much they would buy, and nobody had enough. "Mercy God we have the jam to barter for your butter," said Darrel and Donald's mother when my mother took them our butter on Food Barter Day at school. That was the day Darrel had his hand in a bandage from playing with some jagged scrap metal the boys sneaked down to the end of the tree for the War. I was happy our cow had lots of milk after she got over the shock of the storm. She made us get so much purple jam from Darrel and Donald's mother, we had it on our toast all the time.

The ration points got wrong at McHenry's Store for some days. What happened was the mailman couldn't get through on those days when the giant Douglas fir tree was all over the road from the storm.

Jerry McHenry knew all about the ration points problem before anyone else did, because old J.T. McHenry was his own grandfather.

The mail that didn't come for McHenry's Store was the list of the new points for the foods in the store. Old J.T. McHenry let people have ham slices and Heart's Delight Asparagus and Joan of Arc Kidney Beans and many other foods for the old points, not the new points. The McHenrys didn't find out what they were doing wrong for a whole week. When the government found out McHenry's Store was selling food for wrong ration points, a man came to the store, and he went to the back part where old J.T. McHenry and Jerry McHenry's father had their desks.

Jerry McHenry said the man was from the OPA. That was the Office of Price Ministration. Standing there at old J.T. McHenry's desk the man said it was a disgrace to the War Effort and everybody had to do their share on the Home Front, and if every little store in every little burg set their own prices America would lose the war and Hitler would be here before we knew it, making all the little children speak German.

The OPA man looked up at the photograph on the wall of J.T. McHenry being a hero in the first war. He said anybody who would cheat on the ration points was a disgrace to that uniform up there in that photograph, and he left the store while old J.T. McHenry was still standing halfway between his desk and the photograph on the wall. He just stood there with one hand down on his desk and the other one starting to make some kind of motion, nobody ever knew what motion exactly.

Old J.T. McHenry took it very hard, and he even stayed home from the store for the first time in all his years since the other war.

What happened next was a haunted thing. Old J.T. McHenry took all the sleeping pills they had on the shelves in the store, and he swallowed them with apple cider, and his heart never recovered and he lay in his bed and died right there, never even woke up to say any last words.

And at the funeral everybody dressed up in their church clothes and the minister prayed. "He made this town, Lord. He made this town with his two hands and take him unto your bosom, Lord," said the minister. "Let him not be casted down, he is raised up even now to heaven in the glory of God," he said. And they sang "Comin' in on a Wing and a Prayer," old J.T. McHenry's favorite song.

> Tho' there's one motor gone
> We can still carry on,
> What a show, what a fight,
> Yes, we really hit our target tonight.
> How we sing as we limp thru' the air.
> Look below, there's our field over there.
> With our full crew aboard
> And our trust in the Lord,
> Comin' in on a wing and a prayer.

Then they carried the coffin out of the church and put it on old J.T. McHenry's store truck, and they drove him to the cemetery and put him down in the ground.

Jerry McHenry was famous and he didn't even want to be. He was famous for knowing all what happened about the ration points and old J.T. McHenry being tormented and taking it so hard.

The most mystery part came after, when they found out from old J.T. McHenry's will and testament that the fallen Douglas fir tree behind the playground didn't even belong to the Trout Creek Ridge School. It belonged to old

J.T. McHenry, he let them build the school right beside his property line, and that tree belonged to him all the whole time. He could have sold it for farwood, but he let the school children have it for recess play.

But Shadean was right. There was a hex on that fallen tree, and old J.T. McHenry taking his own life like that proved it.

After the funeral was over and Jerry McHenry came back to school and went back to playing War with the other boys, I pretended I had to go to my cubby and get a handkerchief out of my pencil box. I stood there looking out the window at the fallen tree. Down under the bristly ends of the branches were shadowy places, shapes of things. The hex was in there.

"Everybody fold hands on tables now," said Mrs. Pelley. "Blackout Review time." I walked back to my place and folded my hands.

Something was wrong down there that nobody could see. Down there in those branches lying bent on the ground instead of spreading up in the sky where they belonged. It began when the whole tree plunged down out of the sky with nature being so mixed up. Even the birds and bugs were shocked. Kate and Shadean and Little Peggy and I had been together down there in those shadows. And Ellen too, before. We even took our babies there. All together in our playhouse we had smelled that smell of safe shelter and it wasn't the truth. We just thought we were safe. We weren't safe there, not ever, not even for one minute. We weren't safe from anything at all.

It's January and I've hooked up with a Japanese photo-journalist named Saburo... We have an arrangement: He takes the pictures; I do the talking... My English is far better than his, after all, and English is the best we can do...

REMIND ME

WHAT IS YOUR NAME?

HOW ARE YOU?

WHAT IS YOUR NAME?

Not that English always gets you far, but the kids like the practice, and it's a good idea to get the kids on your side. I smile a lot, tell them my name is Joe, that I am fine, and that usually does the trick, though not always. Two or three times, in other places, kids have chased me off, calling out to each other that I'm a Jew, or picked up stones and fingered them till I've smiled and beamed my way into their little hearts. Kids can be exhausting...

Adults, too. Not that they run after you, giggling and tugging at your sleeve. In a place like this they hang back, staring, sizing up the kind of trouble you might mean. More smiles and greetings in order here. "Salaam Aleekum!" Keep that smile going. "Salaam Aleekum!" Now they're smiling back. Someone hands us a bag of tangerines.

This is Balata, the biggest refugee camp in the West Bank, practically across the road from Nablus. Some Palestinians living here were

79

among the three-quarters of a million who fled or were forced out of what is now Israel in 1948...

Do we need to talk about 1948? It's hardly a secret how the Zionists used rumors, threats, and massacres to expel the Arabs and create new demographics that guaranteed the Jewish nature of Israel.

Of course, it's more comfortable to think of refugees as some regrettable consequence of war, but getting rid of the Palestinians has been an idea kicking around since Theodor Herzl formulated modern Zionism in the late 1800s. "We shall have to spirit the penniless population [sic] across the border," he wrote, "by procuring employment for it in the transit countries, while denying it employment in our own country."

After all, some Zionists reasoned, Palestinians were less attached to their ancestral homeland than the Jews who hadn't lived there for centuries. According to Israel's first prime minister, David Ben-Gurion, a Palestinian "is equally at ease whether in Jordan, Lebanon or a variety of places." With war imminent, Ben-Gurion had no illusions about "spiriting" or inducing the Palestinians away. "In each attack," he wrote, "a decisive blow should be struck, resulting in the destruction of homes and the expulsion of the population." When that was basically accomplished he told an advisor, "Palestinian Arabs have only one role left — to flee."

But if 1948 is no secret, it's all but a non-issue, dismissed entirely by Prime Minister Golda Meir: "It was not as though there was a Palestinian people considering itself as a Palestinian people and we came and threw them out and took their country away from them. They did not exist."

But they did exist, and they do, and here they are... and their children, and their children's children... and still they are refugees... stale ones, maybe, in the nightly news scheme of things, but, nonetheless, refugees... which I suppose means they're waiting to go back...

But back to what? Close to 400 Palestinian villages were razed by the Israelis during and after the '48 war... fleeing Palestinians were declared "absentees" ...their homes and lands declared "abandoned" or "uncultivated" and expropriated for settlement by Jews.

You say refugee camp and I picture tents, people lying on cots... but somewhere along the line Balata's residents figured they'd be here for the long haul, and the camp took on a sort of shabby permanence... People live here, they watch T.V., they shop, they raise families... On first glance, sloshing down a main road, what sets Balata apart is the mud. The snows have melted and the road is mud. Everywhere, mud.

We came here to meet Saburo's friend, but he's gone to a wedding somewhere and won't be back today. Now what? I'm freezing, and I wonder how long we're going to walk around in the cold.

Fortunately someone remembers Saburo from last time he was here and invites us into his shop for tea... ah, tea... holding a cup of tea, that's the ticket for right now... I'm lost in my tea while Saburo arranges a place to spend the night.

Meanwhile, word must be out 'cause small groups of the shebab are coming and going, giving us the once over. Most of them hang out for a few minutes and leave. Foreigners? Journalists? Big deal! We're not the first and won't be the last to drop by looking under their skirts for stories...

One of them, though, maybe he's 16 or 18, takes a shining to me. It must be all my smiling. His English is piss-poor, but that doesn't stop a guy like this, pantomime's not beneath him. He makes it clear he's done some rough-and-tumble with the IDF, the Israeli Defense Forces. He takes out his ID card to prove it. Every Palestinian over 16 in the Occupied Territories has to carry one, and his is green, which means he's done a recent stint in prison. He orders over a friend who sheepishly produces an orange ID, the regular card color for West Bank residents.

"Green card: Intifada!" says my new pal, waving his card... "Orange card: No intifada," he says, holding up his friend's...

Orange Card retreats with a red face while Green Card beams proudly. I beam back, out of sympathy, really, 'cause I've got a bad feeling about a dude without discretion like this... He's destined for a casualty appendix, I'm thinking; he's probably got an appointment with a serious bullet.

Saburo's made arrangements for the night. We'll be staying with someone named Jabril, who speaks pretty good English. Jabril takes us home, sits us down in the front room, makes us comfy. There's full mobilization in the kitchen and he and his brothers bring out one plate after another. It's a regular feast! I tell you, I eat like a king in refugee camps, they pull out all the stops, I blow kisses in the direction of the invisible womenfolk. And now we're stuffed, and Jabril sets up the kerosene heater against our toes, he wants us crispy.

"Coffee?" he asks.

Christ, they love us in Palestine!

Meanwhile, the room's filling with neighbors. They've heard about us and they don't mind answering some questions. I reach for my pad. They've been laughing and talking amongst themselves, but now they're quiet, even the children

they've brought along.
 I ask where they work. "Israel! Israel!" say most. There's jobs in Israel, they say, not in the West Bank. They get up early for their jobs. It's an hour there, an hour back, and they have to be out of the country by 6 p.m. Only Jabril has a local job, in Nablus. The others are part of Israel's convenient low-wage labor pool. Israel calls the economic shots and makes rules to suit itself, as when Defense Minister Rabin said in 1985: "No permits will be given for expanding agriculture or industry [in the Territories] which may compete with the State of Israel."
 Mahmoud says he hasn't worked for two years. He has a green ID card, which means he can't cross into Israel for work. Green card? He was in prison? The soldiers came to his door one day, he says, he asked why and they smashed him in the head! In front of his wife and children! The soldiers wanted to know who was throwing stones. Mahmoud told them it wasn't him, but they took him anyway. He shrugs. "If they don't take me, they'll take you."
 Now they're all blurting stories about soldiers and prisons. Firas says soldiers shot him two years ago and his leg's still not right. Ahmed says soldiers raided his home at midnight, they busted down the door, they came through the roof, they destroyed furniture, they caught him. He was 16. Three years in prison. "For what?" I ask. "For throwing a Molotov cocktail," he says. "And I didn't even see where it landed." The whole crowd busts up. They think that's pretty funny.
 But the Israelis take Molotovs seriously, often demolishing the homes of Molotov throwers. I ask about demolished homes in Balata. They talk it over, pointing different directions, counting on their fingers, naming names.
 "Six houses destroyed by dynamite," Abu Akram announces finally. "One of them belonged to my friend, a butcher, he was a rich man. Eleven other people lived in his house. They had one hour to move." The butcher, it seems, was a collaborator who was discovered and allowed to redeem himself by killing two other collaborators, who were considered dangerous. He killed them; the Israelis put him in prison for life, blew up his home. They say five collaborators have been killed in Balata.
 I ask about life in the camp. "No cinema, no garden," says Jabril. "If the soldier sees me he asks, 'Where

are you going?' If I want to play football in the schoolyard, the soldier comes. So my friends visit my home. We drink tea. We drink coffee. We speak. This is my life."

Jabril says Balata has a reputation with the soldiers. The first West Bank clashes of the intifada occurred here. Jabril says he's been knocked down in Nablus by soldiers who've discovered he's from Balata.

"When I go to Nablus," says Abu Akram, "I go with a hurry and come back. If a soldier stops me, he puts me up against a wall, takes my card, he asks the computer, he asks why I was in prison. If the soldier is very bad, he takes me in a store and beats me. It is best to stay in Balata camp."

We go on the roof. It's freezing up there, but the lights from a nearby Jewish settlement are pretty. It's almost 8 o'clock and the party splits up. No one wants to be caught by soldiers after curfew.

Jabril is exhausted from translating, but the night is still young and he feels an obligation, I suppose, to entertain us. He sets up a video player and we watch 'The Delta Force,' starring Chuck Norris and Lee Marvin. The film is sort of based on a hijacking in the mid-'80s where a U.S. soldier was murdered and several Americans held hostage in Beirut. Eventually the hostages were released. In the movie, however, the Delta Force gets to rescue the hostages à la Entebbe and wipe out scores of Palestinian terrorists to boot. And while the Americans stand together and defiant against their tormentors, the snivelling Palestinians betray their cause en masse when presented with personal harm. Jabril and his brothers mostly watch impassively, shaking their heads from time to time as Palestinians run screaming from battle or are blown to bits by Norris from his rocket-firing motorcycle.

After the video, they prepare mats for us on the floor. Jabril has the couch. He plays a cassette softly to fall asleep to. I recognize the voice — Oum Koulsoum, the Egyptian singer who died years ago. My friend Taha in Cairo told me her funeral was bigger than Sadat's. She wasn't much to look at, sort

OUM KOULSOUM

of like Roy Orbison on a bad day, but what a voice! What a performance! It's obviously a love song... the audience is gasping, I'm gasping, too; I'm like the audience, overwhelmed. The song goes on and on. Jabril flips the cassette. The song is still going.

"What song is this?" I ask. "'Fakarouni,'" Jabril answers; "Remind Me."

Jabril is playing the song for his fiancée in Jordan. She's Palestinian, too, also a refugee... The Israelis won't let her visit because she has no immediate family members left in Palestine to apply for her visa... And Jabril can't go to her. The Israelis won't let him out of the country any more. They accused him of traveling on to Syria on his last visit to Jordan. They accused him of training for terrorist missions with George Habash's Popular Front for the Liberation of Palestine. They accused him of training for terrorist missions in Japan. Japan?... They came for him at night and took him to Nablus prison and interrogated him for two months. They beat him, they kept him from sleeping, they— But we can talk about that some other time, he says. He has to get up early for work.

When Saburo and I wake up, Jabril is already gone... As usual, I'm shivering. The water's too cold to wash with.

This morning we want to check out one of Balata's preparatory schools administered by the United Nations Relief and Works Agency... UNRWA... which tends to

CHUCK NORRIS

some basic needs of Palestinian refugees. We walk to the school but they won't let us in, not without higher authorization. They put me on the phone with the UNRWA area office in Nablus. "You understand we need to take certain security precautions," explains the guy on the other end. "You've seen the situation there." He can give us authorization, if we come in to Nablus. We take the short taxi ride to town and the UNRWA official waves us into his office and dashes off a handwritten pass. We're all set, we're on the UNRWA guest list.

On the way to catch a taxi back to Balata, Saburo gets a wild hair up his ass and decides he's going to get photos of Nablus prison. Nablus prison? With all its barbed wire and watchtowers and guards and "NO PHOTOGRAPHY" signs posted clearly? He gives me all the film he's taken in case soldiers pick him up. And off he goes.

I get to the taxi stand where I see Abu Akram from last night's discussion. He comes over, we shake hands, and then we both notice a soldier in a red beret making his way in our direction. Suddenly, Abu Akram's gone! He and some pals are running through the traffic, and Red Beret's running after them... the Palestinians hop aboard a taxi that's already in motion just as Red Beret is upon them... and Red Beret suddenly gives up his pursuit... maybe it wasn't a pursuit, maybe everyone was out for a run... I don't know... I'm already in a taxi clutching Saburo's film bag, feeling dizzy and like somehow I'm to blame.

Back in Balata, I'm sitting in the headmaster's office and he still won't let me into the school. Like an idiot, I've left my signed permission with an UNRWA dude at an office down the road. Three schoolboys have gone to retrieve it, but they haven't returned, and school's almost out. Come back tomorrow, says the headmaster. Be patient, says the teacher doing the translating. He says Israelis have come into the camp posing as journalists before... they've "interviewed" students and found out who the activists are... then the soldiers have come to make arrests...

Saburo shows up about the time the bell ends the school day. We step outside and are surrounded by kids asking our names and religions, which we answer several times... The teacher comes out of the office and shoos them away... He's joined by a colleague and they agree to show us around, permission or not.

They take us to a classroom. No electricity, no

87

heat, they say, it's been like this for 40 years.
"They thought the school was temporary when they built it," says one. "They thought they'd go back to their homes [in Israel] in a year or two." UNRWA is

promising electricity, he says, but the students had to strike for it. They show us where the rain drips into the classroom. They show us the outdoor toilets whose walls have crumbled.

The headmaster appears, he has angry words for the teachers. The three of them step aside, arguing, apparently, on the advisability of talking to "journalists." The teachers are raising their voices. The headmaster walks off

89

sullenly. The teachers rejoin us. "Never mind," one of them says. "We told him we take full responsibility."

They tell us their curriculum corresponds to Jordan's. The Israelis allow English and math books in from Jordan, they say, but no history or geography text, for example, that mentions Palestine. Not that it matters, says one teacher. "Since the intifada it is not necessary to teach such children that this is not Israel."

They say soldiers pass by ... soldiers chase people through the school ... they shoot ... it doesn't make for a good school environment for the 500 boys. What about for teachers? On a recent morning, says one of them, on his way to school, soldiers beat him.

They ordered him to take down a picture of Arafat from a wall. Yes, but why did they beat him? "For speaking to them in English and not in Hebrew," he says.

Saburo and I make a quick visit to the local UNRWA clinic. They don't ask for authorization here. A nurse gives us a tour of the antenatal department — 50 camp births a month, she says; the laboratory; the rehabilitation unit; and (with some pride) the new X-ray room.

Now the doctor will see us.

The nurse jumps us past the long line waiting at his door. The doctor greets us into his office and shoos out a couple of female patients.

Just two doctors serve the clinic, he says, one of them a relief doctor. "The main problem," he says, "is overload." The clinic gets up to 300 patients a day. (Last night, at the roundtable discussion, the men joked about the rushed diagnoses at the clinic. "Go to the window! Go to the window!" they sang, mimicking the staff sending them away with hurried prescriptions.)

The doctor says he sees a lot of respiratory illnesses from bad ventilation and overcrowding, "from problems related to political and social conditions."

Meanwhile, there's knocking on the door! We've been too long! The women who've been kicked out want back in! Whose clinic is it, anyway?

Outside we find Green Card — Mr. Intifada from yesterday — and a friend. They've come to fetch us. For what? Their English isn't good enough to explain. We follow them. I've become familiar with Balata's main roads, but they lead us into the maze of side streets, into the back alleys, where there's hardly a couple of shoulder-widths between houses and little boys are playing marbles ... We're twisting and turning... hopping over open drainage canals...going left, going right, going in circles, I can't tell. Periodically Green Card motions for us to stop, peers around a corner, motions for us to follow. "Police danger," he informs us. He stops us again. They frisk us. They go through our belongings. Green Card turns the pages of my passport, he studies leftover bank receipts from Cairo, my air ticket, my camera... He's flipping through my journals... He's serious, grim even... Of course, I could have reams of notes about a hot-tubbing experience with Ariel Sharon and Green Card wouldn't have a clue ... In any case, they decide we're kosher... more twists and turns... we're back on a muddy main street ... whew...

Now we're in a house, the tea is coming... Jabril is there, and a few faces from the night before... but there's someone new... you'd figure after all the precautions Green Card took we'd be meeting Arafat himself or at least a Black Panthers guerrilla, but this new fellow looks pretty ordinary... and his spiel isn't anything I haven't heard before... He's vague about who he is, though, and I don't press him for a resume.

He says the uprising is the result of years of suffering, that the intifada started spontaneously but is now directed by the PLO. He says the intifada focused world attention on the Palestinians and now there's a chance for a political solution...

That's the tip-off. This guy's with Fateh, Arafat's faction of the PLO... I've made a game of guessing what PLO faction a Palestinian supports by his opinion of the "peace process"... Popular Front supporters, for example, oppose the talks 'cause of stiff Israeli preconditions on the Palestinian negotiating team.

He says Balata is mainly with Fateh. Fateh supports the negotiations, so he supports the negotiations ...but he's a skeptic. "The majority of Israelis don't want land-for-peace," he says. "They want to make agreements with other Arab nations, but not with Palestinians." What does he see ahead? "More settlements, more soldiers, more [Jewish] immigration." And if the negotiations fail, then what? "What do you expect?" he says. "The intifada will continue."

The discussion's over. The women are sending in food. We're dipping pita bread into all kinds of stuff. We're off politics now. We're laughing. Here comes the coffee...

They're asking Saburo about Japan, and I turn his rough English into English they can understand. It comes out that Saburo is something of a spiritualist, he reads lifelines... Green Card pulls his chair up and sticks out his palm. After a little analysis, Saburo has complimentary words about Green Card's emotions and intelligence... Then Saburo looks hard at the palm and announces that something will happen to Green Card soon. "Back in jail," says Jabril and they all laugh. "No," insists Saburo, "things will get better."

They warn us about the upcoming strikes... Hamas, the Islamic fundamentalist group, has called a general strike for tomorrow; the Unified National Leadership has called one for the day after; and both groups have called for a strike the day after that ... That's going to mess up the taxi situation. We decide to split rather than get stranded in Balata.

We take a taxi to Nablus ...the Nablus streets are all but empty; maybe there's a curfew coming up ...At the taxi stand we find a Jerusalem-bound stretch Mercedes and wait inside with a couple and their boy. The driver won't leave till he gets one or two more passengers, but we'll have to leave soon if we want to get through Ramallah before Ramallah's five o'clock curfew...

A jeep pulls up across the street. Soldiers jump out and head into a narrow Old City passageway. There's a gunshot... Another jeep pulls up. More soldiers. A soldier with a radio drops his phone and it swings wildly out of reach below his knees. He can't seem to get at it. He's having trouble. The boy in the taxi is laughing, calling the soldier "mignoon" — crazy. His father says to roll up the windows in case there's gas... Another jeep shows up. More soldiers are piling out and ducking into the passageway.

And finally we're leaving Nablus... past the prison ...We're leaving Balata behind ...Balata is receding... I'm looking forward to the long, winding hilly stretch ahead... Jerusalem is one hour away... Jerusalem is one hour away... meanwhile, I'll enjoy the scenery.

A Few Reservation Notes on Love and Hunger

Sherman Alexie

James Earl Alexie, age thirteen, is my little brother. Actually, he's my second cousin, but my parents adopted him as an infant because his natural mother, Jackie, couldn't raise him. Jackie had four kids by three different fathers before she was twenty-one years old. It's a sad story, I suppose, of this baby who nearly starved to death because his mother didn't have enough sense to even feed herself. James also had two brothers and a sister who were sent out to foster homes, but they've since been returned to their natural mother. We kept James, however, despite Jackie's attempts to regain custody. Still, he does visit his natural family often and we've never tried to hide his past from him.

In fact, James spends a significant amount of time with his natural family. He visits them in a house so dirty that I refuse to enter it. James has come back from his visits with head lice on more than one occasion. Even now, I can feel my head itch and I wonder how it makes James feel. I wonder if he dreams about those lice, about hunger, about abandonment, about survival.

James is currently in the seventh grade at Reardan Junior High School in Reardan, Washington, a mostly white town thirty miles from the Spokane Indian Reservation. I also attended Reardan Junior and Senior High School, but I was actually the only Indian during my first year there. By the time I graduated, there were still only five of us. There are now two or three Indians in every grade at Reardan.

∿∿∿

Sherman: James, you're half-white, quarter-black, and quarter-Indian. What does that mean to you?

James: I never really thought of it. It's an everyday thing.

But all of your friends are white, right?

Yeah.

How do you think they feel about it? How do you feel about being Indian in such a white world?

I have to cope with it. I have to be with white people my whole life. I have to get used to it, I guess. They respect me for being Indian. I have to respect them for being white.

Do your white friends know you're part black?

No.

Do your Indian friends know you're part black?

No.

∿∿∿

I remember James' natural father, Dale. He was white and at least ten years older than me. He seemed much older, in fact, but I realize now that he was only eighteen or so. I remember that Jackie and Dale came to visit us when she was pregnant with James. Jackie stayed inside the house and talked with my parents while Dale stayed outside and played with me and my brother and sisters.

I remember that Dale suddenly picked me up in a bear hug and squeezed my chest until I couldn't breathe, until I passed out from lack of oxygen. While I was unconscious, he dropped me to the ground and I scraped my face. I was only eight years old and couldn't fight Dale. My brother and sisters couldn't do much, either. My brother was only a couple years older than me, and my sisters were a year younger. All they could do was wait for me to wake up. All they could do was carry me over to the garden faucet and wash my face, while Dale laughed and laughed. I remember that he kept telling me that I wasn't hurt. I remember that he kept telling me that I was a big baby.

James has never even met his natural father.

∿∿∿

How does it feel to live on the reservation and go to school at a white school like Reardan?

Kids on the rez are bad. They tease me about going to a white school. They're ignorant. They go to Indian school and they expect everything I do to be white because I go to a white school.

How do white people in Reardan feel about you being from the rez?

The kids don't mind. A few teachers are prejudiced.

How do you feel about those teachers?

They make me mad. They treat the Indians different than the rest.

Do you think that's going to change?

It's an everyday aspect of the rest of my life. There's always going to be racists.

∿∿∿

James was always hungry when he first came to us. As a baby, he ate and drank more than any of us did as adolescents. He always reminded me about how much more I had. Even though I'd also grown up in poverty, I had never starved. My parents always found some way to feed me and my siblings.

"I never really thought about it," my sister Kim said when I asked her how she felt about James' hunger.

"How come?" I asked.

"I don't know."

I wonder how much of our own hunger any of us remember. I remember that we didn't starve. But I also remember that we rarely had seconds. I remember that my sisters used to scrape all of the food that had dropped off our plates during meals into a big pile and scoop it into their mouths.

"You liar," my sisters tell me now. "We never did that."

My parents don't remember that happening either, but my brother and I remember. We laughed about it then. We laugh about it now. But it hurts, too, way down deep in a place that I cannot reach or describe.

I wonder if James remembers his hunger, but I'm scared to ask him. If he doesn't remember, I'll wonder why I remember my lesser hungers so well. If he does remember, it'll break my heart.

∽∽∽

Here's a dumb question. What do you want to be when you grow up?
What do you want to be when you grow up?
Good one. Now, seriously?
Play basketball in college and the NBA. Be a lawyer. Teacher. It's something I'll find out later.
Can you be anything you want to be?
Pretty much, except for pro sports. That's one in a million. I guess if I try as hard as I can, maybe I can make it to college to play sports.
What if you don't make it in sports? There were only three Indians playing Division I basketball last year and none in the NBA.
I know the odds aren't with me. Be a lawyer, I guess.
Why a lawyer?
I think I'd do good at it. It's the type of qualities I have. I argue good. I figure out problems easily. Mysteries. I figure a book out good. There's nothing else I'm good at, like drawing or being a doctor, etc.
That's not true. You're good at a lot of things.
Not really.

∽∽∽

James plays basketball at the same school where I was a star. But James doesn't always get to play during his junior high games. I had my name and face in the newspapers for years. I got headlines. But James sits at the end of the bench and holds back tears.

I went to a game of his recently and knew that he wanted to play for me. I knew he wanted to get into the game and make a good shot or pass. He stared up at me out of the corner of his eye during most of the game. Occasionally, during huddles, he'd look right at me and shrug his shoulders. I'd point at his coach and tell him to pay attention.

James' coach, Dan Graham, was also one of my coaches during my playing days. He was and is a loud and aggressive man, competitive to a fault, temperamental, and unforgiving of mistakes. I loved Coach; I love him now.

"You get that ball," Coach yelled at me more than once. "Be a shooter. Toughen up. Get in the program or you'll be sitting right beside me."

I loved it. I threw myself to the floor, dove into the stands after loose balls, slammed my slight body against the bodies of bigger boys, and loved it. I played basketball with all my love and rage and hunger. I was good. But, of course, I was just a good high school player. I knew I'd never be more than a role player for some small college team, and the NBA was completely out of the question.

"It's your game," Coach yelled at me. "Take it to the hoop."

I was in love, in love. I held that ball in my hands and faked left, right, up, and then drove for the hoop, just like coach demanded. I left the floor, held that ball on my fingertips, and took the shot. I won games; I lost games. I played.

But James didn't play. He sat at the end of the bench, always close to tears. I can always tell when he's near tears. He and I are alike in many ways. His face looks much like mine does whenever I'm close to tears, but we cry for different reasons.

I cried whenever we lost basketball games; James cries because he doesn't even get to play.

"I don't think he's going to be all that good," I said to my older brother Arnold as we drove around the reservation.

"Left-handers can hardly ever play basketball," Arnold said. He was a much more talented basketball player than I ever was, but struggled with his weight and discipline.

"I hope he gets better," I said. "I know it hurts him not to play. Especially when we're at the games."

"He's got time."

"Yeah," I said. "I forget that he's actually not a genetic Alexie."

My father was a great high school basketball player. He was also a pretty good old man basketball player. I couldn't beat him one-on-one until my sophomore year in high school.

"Yeah," Arnold said. "Maybe James ain't like us genetically, but he grew up with us."

You had it easier than both your natural siblings and your adopted siblings. What do you think about that?

I feel bad in some aspects. At my (natural) mom's there are really poor kids who come around.

There are a lot of poor kids on the rez, aren't there?

Yeah.

How does that make you feel?

Lucky. Knowing I wouldn't have to need anything. Don't have to worry about food, shelter, stuff like that. I don't have to worry about my next meal or working or feeding myself. I have stuff other kids don't.

Other Indians? And whites?

Yeah.

Are you racist?

For the whites in some aspects. I take it personal when I hear people say we don't deserve stuff. When a teacher says something that's not true. When a teacher said we (Indians) gave them diseases. Their ancestors were mean. They killed us.

What teacher said that? When?

Miss — in fifth grade.

How did that make you feel as an Indian?

Bad, because it was mostly other white kids who learned that and thought it was true. We were always the bad people.

So you were worried that the white kids would believe her?

Yeah, I was afraid. I wanted to tell the truth. Set the truth out. I wanted them knowing that it wasn't us who brought all the diseases.

Did you tell your friends the truth? During or after class?

Yeah, during class. I raised my hand. Challenged the teacher and told the truth. That they brought all the diseases that killed. They brought measles, chickenpox, smallpox. If it wasn't for us, they'd be dead. Columbus would've died without the Indians.

How did the teacher respond?

She really didn't answer. I think she knew she was wrong.

Did you like her?

No. She was a pretty good teacher, in some aspects. She can only teach whites, and she's prejudiced. Prejudiced people shouldn't teach because they teach the Indian kids different.

> How many Indians were in your class?
> Three. Me, John, Justin.
> How do you get along with them?
> Good.
> Are you best friends?
> Yeah, I guess you could say that.
> Are they better friends than your white friends?
> Yeah, in some aspects.

James sat down at a table across from me. I handed him a copy of a William Carlos Williams poem:

> This Is Just To Say
>
> I have eaten
> the plums
> that were in
> the icebox
>
> and which
> you were probably
> saving
> for breakfast
>
> Forgive me
> they were delicious
> so sweet
> and so cold

I asked James to write me a poem like that. He asked me what I meant. I told him to write a poem about being sorry and not sorry. He struggled for a while and then handed me his poem:

I'm sorry
that there's no
food
in the house.

I'm sorry I'm broke.

I'm sorry for everything.

I'm sorry for nothing.

What about girls? When I was there at Reardan I got treated differently by girls. They didn't pay much attention to me. How about you?

We're all pretty good friends. There's not much romantic stuff. And I don't like any of the girls that way. They're pretty but not the type I'm looking for. I want smart, good attitude, the type that likes school. Somebody who would have a job. They'd be able to take care of me, too, and I'd take care of them if they get hurt or something.

Are you interested in white or Indian or black girls?

White, mostly. There's very few pretty Indians my age. And a few blacks I like who are older.

A lot of Indian women don't like Indian men going out with white women. What do you think? What do you think of me marrying an Indian women?

If you like her, that's good. But it wouldn't really matter what I think. It's your decision.

There are so few Indians, do you feel an obligation to stay with Indians, to make sure we survive?

I thought of that, but it's kind of hard. I would have to marry a full-blood Indian. If I looked for an Indian woman, I'd have to carry a family tree around. You wouldn't know if you were related or not.

Define love for me.

Something two people have for each other. Something they like about each other. The kind of people they are — funny, serious, orderly-type thing.

That's romantic love. How about family love?

The type of love in a family. That's to keep them together. Something that makes them a family and not strangers. A bond.

You were adopted, how does that make you feel?

Makes me wonder why I was the only one given up. I'm lucky considering how they live, my (natural) brothers and sister. They don't have much order. They don't have much respect for adults in what they say. But then, it's mostly adults' fault. They don't set good examples. They took too long to take order. My (natural) mom messed up. They already grew up with dirty bedrooms, not cleaning up after themselves.

How do you feel about your natural brothers and sister? Your natural mom?

That when I see them, they're a lot the same. I like them. I was there, but I'm not there. I love them still. Same as my adopted family.

So you're in a unique situation, but lots of Indians have been raised by family members. You're kind of traditional, you know? How do you feel about Indian tradition?

I like it. It's unique. The language is confusing. How they say it and stuff. White people don't have a tradition. They don't remember their ancestors. We always remember our ancestors. Talk about them. Live like they did in some aspects. Carry on tradition.

You grass dance. Why?

It's fun. I can't dance any other way. It's kind of easy. You have to set boundaries. When I grow up I want to know something about my heritage, where I came from.

Do you want to keep living on the reservation?

No. Hopefully, when I grow up I get to see new places. Travel, see a lot of stuff. It's not a good life to stay on the rez. There's nothing about it. All you see are drunks.

That's really depressing, isn't it?

You see the rez and you see how it's run. They never try anything new. They never build anything good. All they build is a bingo casino. They're finally trying to build a youth center where kids can do something, instead of nothing. Keep them away from drugs and drinking and smoking.

What do you think of the future for Indians?

It ain't turning out good. They won't leave the rez.

They stay there forever. They don't care about their heritage. They don't go to culture camp.

But it's not all their fault, is it?

No. It's their house. How they grew up and everything. I think it's mostly the white people making life so easy. The stuff makes them lazy. When they go to school they don't have to work hard and do nothing.

Is it ever going to be good for Indians?

Probably not, the way we're going. I don't think it will be any better.

∿∿∿

James runs up to me and gives me a hug every time he sees me. I miss those hugs whenever I'm away from him. He misses me, I think.

I used to believe his life was much better than mine. I've found how many of the same things we believe. James has his own fears and dreams, his own pain and sorrows. As a writer, I suppose I wanted to get inside his head, to see with his eyes. I can't. I can only pretend to. I can only ask him questions and hope I'm not leading him someplace I want him to go. I hope this story is about him and not about me, but I think it's about both of us. I hope he will always love me.

Just like for all the rest of us, James' years have been hard, and reservation years are really like dog years. James isn't thirteen; he's ninety-one.

∿∿∿

What's your favorite book?

Mystery books.

What's your favorite music?

All types.

Your favorite food?

I don't really have nothing.

Are you hungry now?

Yeah.

What?

A cheeseburger and fries.

Photos by Marly Stone

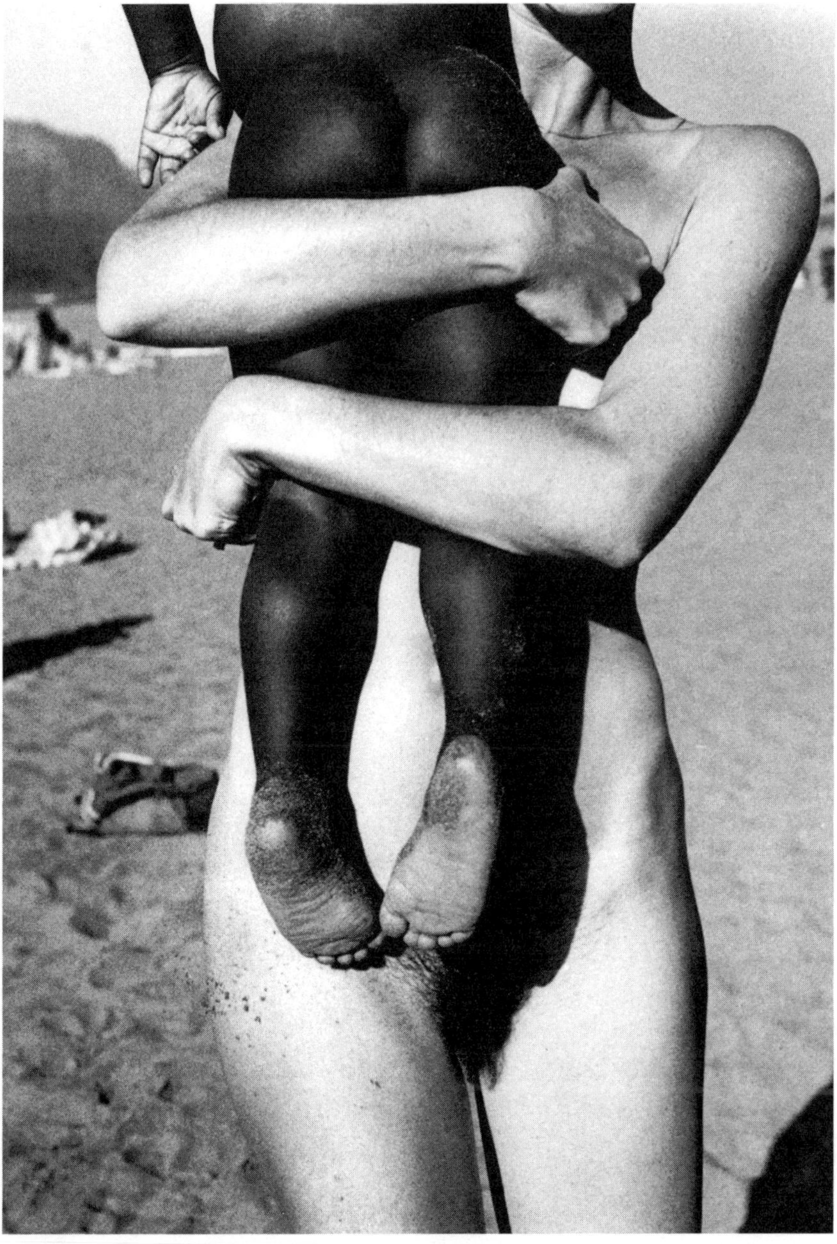

Excerpt #2 from

The Kingdom at Hand

David Axelrod

Sitting cross-legged in red volcanic ash,
my son, who just learned to read and write,
bends over his journal, taking notes, waiting
for me to climb the switchbacks that separate us.

In his bright green sweater he is like
one of those young ponderosa pines that fall
as seeds from the canyon rim, where forested
high desert plateau crowds the abrupt edge.
Seeds fall like an amber, whirling rain,
land on narrow ledges, and, after thunderstorms,
sprout in an inch of duff and dust, the pale
taproots tendrilling into damp granite.

Reaching him, I ask to hear what he's written.
Each sentence is in future tense! Beginning,
"Tomorrow we will" and ending, "it will be fun!"

I explain the present tense, but he rolls his eyes.
It's too plain-spoken and bland! It's no use
talking about how longing slanders our lives
and makes us poor. This meal we eat today
never satisfies so much as a promised feast.

Two years ago, illiterate, he would sit,
bent over drawings he'd name only after
they were complete: "Beewa Soars Witchery,"
or "What Swallows See at Night." He'd scribble
madly all over a sheet of paper, then recite:
"Lightening cut through the air, the Immoral
Sword of Baladorn! Claps of hot air from deep
dungeons of thunder! And the Windy Queen came,
matting down cornstalks with her flying cape,
and squash crawled leafy through the straw!"

Now there's a caution before every word,
a pause of doubt that blurs instinct.
What did they teach him in school that he might
spend his entire lifetime trying to forget,
the way every man who limps, after years
of slogging behind, for an hour forgets
his old shame and suddenly abandoned,
traipses with child-like shrieks of grace?

In the hallways at his school, which smell
of sour milk and paste, hang rows of identical
cottonball clouds. And there are mosaics
of George Washington, "The Father of Our Country,"
and "President of Our Dollar," spelled out
in very pink kidney beans. His eyes are black
turtle beans. He smiles (so much as a slave-owner
with wooden teeth smiled) a mouthful of northern
navy beans. And his ears are giant limas!

Thumb-tacked on the wall opposite one room
are twenty-three leafless trees, each brown
trunk standing isolated in a smudge of watery
blue and green, and in the upper left-hand
corner, a small, amorphous slice of a once
golden orb casts its dimmer light to earth.

Put Out to Sea

Matthew Stadler

I told my father I'd like to put out to sea on a freighter, the summer when I was fifteen, to spend six years on the earth's open oceans and not pass them locked up in the secondary schools and the university.

I had read books about sailors and heard the ship's steam whistles blowing in the harbor. I would sit by the shore and watch them grow more and more distant, their horn blasts diminished down to ghostly whispers, barely audible among the calling of seabirds. I was a foolish boy intoxicated by the cheap romanticism of the sailor's life, the seductive lure of peril and isolation, the promise of discovery, exotic ports, and friendship. There was a drawing in my *Golden Treasury of the World's Oceans* which showed two young sailors sharing the watch on a black Indonesian night. They were perched high above the ship's deck, reclining in a small nest, pressed together, gazing into the night. The curve of the earth's edge was visible where it met the sky. It was all I ever wanted. The nearness and warmth of a friend sharing that privileged view.

There were several months during which I made plans, regarding this fantasy as a real alternative. I plotted out a means to realize it, with or without my family's blessing. It was the year after Herman had left, and I was very soured on the old district. The energy and time I'd spent on that obsession was free to be turned to my new plan of escape. I acquired pamphlets by mail from shipping companies whose names I'd seen at the loading docks. Pamphlets about anything: shipping prices, storage techniques, yearly stock reports (so I'd be familiar with the whole operation). In the afternoons I watched the boats, sitting on a bench by the municipal pier, or sometimes from a clearing up on the bluffs. I never spoke with a sailor or a captain, or with anyone for that matter. My plans were top secret and were only finally revealed when I took my father into my confidence.

I gathered my courage and said one night that I was going to sea and what did he think. We were sitting together in the front parlor, a bright fire dancing and spitting on the irons. My stomach was all butterflies and nervous, wondering what he'd say now that I'd let my secret out.

"What was that?" he asked, looking up from his lecture notes.

"I'm leaving school, to go to sea," I said quite boldly. I hadn't the slightest idea what I wanted from him, except perhaps, simply his attention. He stared at the black windows, our reflections wrapped and warped along the old, sagging glass. I waited, patient as a teakettle boiling.

"It's quite costly, I understand. Even the fares for children."

"But I'm not going as a passenger, Daddy, I'm going as a sailor." He looked up at me.

"What an idea...to sea as a sailor. I read a book about that once, a boy about your age running off to the piers at Southampton, finding himself work on a steam ship." He drifted away into his reverie.

"But I'd like really to do it, Daddy, now." He cocked his head to one side and began drumming on the tabletop. I fidgeted in my seat and wondered how to proceed.

"Such a good story it would make, a boy like you going off to sea in a modern ship. There's such a lot of characters on these ships, I imagine, each with a host of stories to tell. What a fine idea for a book."

"I'm sure I could keep a diary."

He nodded. "Or perhaps as a memoir."

"But I've not gone yet."

110   "Of course you haven't, you're only still just a boy, after all."

"But I want to go, soon."

"You wouldn't mind if I try this out on some friends, would you?"

"Try what out?"

"Your little story idea, see what they think."

"Couldn't you just tell me what *you* think, tell me if you'll help me?"

"What sort of help could I give you?"

"Well." I really didn't know (though I *did* know this slim thread of his attention was something to cling to). "Well, just, first, talk to me about it because I don't know what I'm doing really, yet, and then help me to figure out exactly *what* to do."

"Yes, yes, of course. I think more reading would be a good idea, as preparation."

"I've done a lot of reading already." I pointed out. "Books and pamphlets and technical manuals."

"All of that?" He seemed impressed.

"But when should I actually go to sea, Daddy, when do you think I can leave school and do it?"

"You don't really want to leave school, do you?"

"Well, I..." The simplicity of his question made it doubly hard to answer. I knew that in fact I didn't really want to go, but also that I did not want simply to stay. I wanted to be prevented from going. I wanted to be forced back to school, made to attend against my adventurous will. "I don't want to leave school, no."

"There's so much to be learned in school," he added, touching me with his strange hand.

"But, Daddy, I don't just want to stay either." The difficult fact came lumbering out, a bitter metal chain that I hoped would — by virtue of its nakedness and truth — link me securely to his attention. Already I could sense him drifting away. "I want to run away," I added urgently, "even though I also want to be in school."

"That makes no sense," he informed me, rising from his chair. "Either you want to be in school or you don't. And I'm happy to hear it's the former." I lay down across both our chairs, filling the empty space he'd just left. I was dizzy and a bit short of breath. My father continued. "Could you maybe find an assignment that allows you to pursue this nautical interest within the boundaries set by school?"

(Intimacy was such a terribly difficult thing for me then. I groped and grabbed for it in my clumsy adolescent way, completely stupid about other people's minds and perceptions. Just when I felt certainly on the verge of a kiss, an embrace, or some warm word and tears, my moment would turn upside down, dumping cold showers of indifference upon me. I was forever repeating, in some variation, the terrible experience I'd had on the verge of puberty when I was invited to my first sleep over. In the absolute darkness of the basement room where we'd all camped out in sleeping bags, I had complied with the announced plan that we all undress and work our little bodies up to an erotic pitch so the lights could be turned on and all of us could see each other, thus sealing our bond forever. I'd cast off everything, including my socks, and was playing my hands all over my body to a pitch of delight when, at the call of the unbearably stimulating countdown from ten, we arrived at "the moment" and the lights came brightly on, revealing a room full of pajamaed boys and me, alone, naked and erect among them. I withered and shrank, jumping back into my bag to hide, and never forgave them the betrayal.)

It was like that with my father in the moment I've just described. By slow and secret signals I'd been beckoned to let him look inside me, to reveal myself as an offering to seal our bond. The confessional urge has always held, for me, that seduction. If (I kept believing) I revealed myself, some important link would thereby be forged.

Locating the object of revelation has proven more and more impossible as I've grown older. My body no longer contains me. To be naked is not enough, is, in fact, counterproductive. I am unreadable without my costume. Sometimes I long for that impossibly distant condition, the one which my cruel peers exploited, where the unbuttoning of a shirt, the tugging down of an elastic waistband, could mean so terribly much. Now it means nothing. We routinely strip for doctors without any of the intimacy and terror we knew as children. There is nothing now my body holds which can be meaningfully revealed. It is a greater horror to be caught wearing the wrong outfit than to be seen naked.

I followed my father's insensitive advice and found ways to incorporate school and my fascination with sailors. Primarily I found that I might gain some satisfaction by attending school in a sailor's suit and hat. By this conceit I felt enclosed within my longing and at the same time was denied its consummation. I was a sailor forced to attend school. This fact was announced at every moment simply by virtue of my costume. I had no need to say a thing about it.

Cereus Blooms at Night

Shani Mootoo

A group of boys stoops huddled in a circle peering into its center, heads locked together like a mass of papaya seeds blocking the light out. In science studies yesterday the class of boys and girls learned about the reflexes of plants — that they respond favorably to music and to being talked to and show signs of trauma when placed close to flames.

Candlelight flickers yellow across their concentrating faces. One of them holds the lit candle first about one foot away, then gradually draws closer to a praying mantis that is gripped between a pair of lab tweezers.

The insect tenses its torso and rubs its front legs up and down swiftly. The boys are fascinated that they can effect such reaction from the bug. Their bodies tingle with excitement. "Go closer. Slow down, na. Not so fast!" commands one of them. As the flame gets nearer, the insect's body begins to arch unnaturally, the head twists, and the front legs blur in frantic speed. The instant the flame touches a back leg, all movement stops abruptly. The chitinous body glows where the flame touches, crackling and hissing as sparks spit and sputter. The abdomen takes the longest to disintegrate, but the boys don't give up. One of them holds the remainder of the torso with the tweezers as another torches more persistently. When, eventually, the head falls off like the tip of a spent match, one boy reaches into his jar and pulls out a grasshopper for its turn.

∿∿∿

After school this same band of boys reluctantly heads home. Walking side by side across the entire road, moving just barely enough for a car to pass only when it is inches away from them and the infuriated driver impatiently rests on the horn, the boys turn a fifteen minute trip into an hour's adventure. All the way to their homes they chain-kick pebbles that have worked themselves out of the grip of the spongy asphalt, trying to see whose chain would remain unbroken longest. In a suitably flat area in the middle of the road, where there are three potholes of varying sizes, they stop to pitch marbles. One of them uses the edge of his callused bare hand to dust the four-foot-square area to perfect smoothness and then empties his little cloth pouch of dazzling prized marbles onto the road to entice and make the others jealous. "Anybody could buy a pretty marble, but not just anybody could pitch," they challenge back. They stop further along to pelt ripe pomme cytheres, more for the thrill of being able to effect the fall of one, than for the pleasure of sucking on one. Better yet, they pelt the black birds that, mesmerized by the fermenting sweetness of the juices, cling to the fruit even upside down, oblivious to the callous desires beneath them.

And the boys pretend to be oblivious to the girls straggling behind them, holding each others' hands, telling secrets and giggling.

∿∿∿

Two from the same school, a girl and a boy, fall outside of any of the several cliques (imposed on them, at first, followed later by their own choice). If two might constitute a clique, they have formed their own, not because she wants his company, but because it is easier to ignore jeers and whispering when fortified by the presence of at least one other person. She carries a hierarchy of her own where there are those few outcasts with whom she avoids association. (No point in ensuring double ostracism — and besides if they are so undesirable, she reasons, why should she want to have them as her friends?) Using filters of her own design, she came to the conclusion that he is the least intolerable of the handful of wandering outcasts. They are each others' buffers in the schoolyard.

When students taunt him that he and she are girlfriend and boyfriend he blushes peevishly, but inside he is delighted at the attention and acknowledgment of their "relationship." She, on the other hand, is adept at redirecting his amorous attentions. Rather than lose her closeness he barters for favors, here a rub, there a rub, which she grants for fear of being bossy or unfeeling.

She gets him to accompany her on the shiny silver mucous trails that lead to bulbous, buff periwinkle snails, alive and ripe for the torture squad's delights. One clean blow with a heavy gym boot would shatter the periostracum into a loosely glued, gooey green, yellow, and pink jigsaw puzzle of its former shell. He complies with her messianic collecting of the snails in plastic bags. Once the bags are stretched and weighted beyond capacity, they carry them down to the backyard fence and turn the bags out over the fence to deliver the gastropods out of reach of the schoolyard's bullies. He waits patiently for his turn while the snails are safely disposed of.

He prods and nudges her away from the wire fence through which snails are already crawling back into the yard. Peculiarly, he likes to do it wherever he might cause a scene, or shock. Wherever someone might see him. He guides her to the back wall quivering with the flattened shadows of a tamarind tree. High up the moldy, cracking concrete wall, through half-open aluminum jalousies, shrieks and screams of unfettered after-school wildness stoke his pubescent desire. Joking, teasing, touching, he leans his pudgy body into hers pinning her like a butterfly to the cool wall, and he rubs his hand up and down the front of her white school blouse.

It is a relatively small club growing in his pant leg, she notices, that is starting to press into her thigh. Mala throws her head back and giggles, more high-pitched than usual. She dips, ducks down, spins around and swiftly maneuvers out of his clumsy embrace. He waits, unsure yet grinning, looking to her for a firm refusal, or for further encouragement. She runs back to him, grabs his hand, tugging him along with her, and says, "Let's go to your house. Your bedroom."

Biting the corner of his lip, he tries to yank her to a halt, protesting that they will be alone, that his mother won't be home until much, much later in the evening. Of course, you idiot, Mala says and continues, if she were there they couldn't do it anyway — she'd kill then. Mala is close to the truth in spite of the exaggeration. Being alone terrifies him, dissipates the desire. He turns to face the corner of the building, towards the front yard. He grazes a grubby shoulder along the length of moldy back wall as he hesitantly limps away from her, pouting, his eyes cast on the damp concrete littered with raw, pink, wet-weather earthworms all around his feet.

Mala catches up with him before he rounds the corner. She traps him against the wall, grabs his wrist, and pushes a reluctant fist inside her opened white school blouse. The fist disintegrates, weakened by its brush against the silky soft, padded cup of breast. Fingers extend, explore, and mold themselves around the little hump. His other hand gropes behind her, discovering another mound for its own pleasure. Squeals of wildness accentuate through the jalousies, and the sight of a flash of royal-blue schoolgirl uniform about to round the corner — but its direction abruptly changes in mid-flight — adds fuel to this moment for him. If only someone can see him now. Aroused beyond control he shoves his open mouth, tongue first, like a can opener, towards Mala's mouth. She thumps a firm palm against his chest, and says, "Not here, let's go to your house...I want to do it with you."

༺ ༻

In the opposite direction from Mala's house, they take his usual short cut across the golf course, and there he tries to hold her hand. She squeezes his hand and releases it dismissively, plopping her books in his. She skips ahead down through a row of poui trees that mark the edge of the golf course, leaving him several paces behind. Mala seems to know his route better than he.

He follows her across a foul-smelling ravine of stagnant, thick, black water where they beat through swarms of mosquitoes, curtains of black flies, to the back of his house.

Inside his yard she defers to his lead. He stops to watch a dragonfly skim the surface of rain water that has collected in half of a rusting oil drum of wriggling mosquito larvae. She wants to hurry him on, but he dilly-dallies by the regimented row of old, peeling banana trees, wanting to show her his multiplying-by-the-minute brood of rabbits in a rickety hutch that he constructed himself, he boasts.

Mala tugs at his shirt sleeve, insisting that they go straight up to his room.

He leaves the bedroom door ajar. Mala shuts it. He goes straight to his homework desk and busies himself twirling his compass around his protractor. She stands behind him, not at all caring for any sense of his body, but intent on keeping him attuned to what has now become *her* goal. She braces herself and rustles her fingers in his greasy hair, runs them up and down his damp, hot neck, flitting one in and around an oily ear. He utters: "Do...do...you know...did you see...Joyce and Gillian? Did you see them copying from each other? In chemistry today? They could get caught, you know! What if they get caught?"

Mala moves away, remaining behind his back. He arranges the messy pile of books on his desk to deny sounds of her undressing. He leafs through a biology text, not really seeing the black and white reproductions of red ants.

She stands at the side of his desk without her shirt, without her bra, and without her school skirt, waiting for him to look up. At the edges of his vision he sees bare skin and the worn elastic band of panties just over the rim of his desk. He turns, mesmerized by her deep cinnamon swirl of navel. Slowly he adjusts his burning eyes to rest first on one pale brown breast, and then on the other. He pushes his chair back and rises to face her. She holds his hand and pulls him to his bed as he takes quick glances to the door, aroused one moment, stricken with panic the next — the panic of the judgementless and witnessless moment.

Mala lies down in his too soft bed, and complete with his running shoes — he remains fully clothed in his high school uniform — he climbs on, guided by her, hovering and trembling and frightened and bumbling over her practically naked body. He stays propped up, elevated, on his knees and elbows. When his fear succumbs to an urgent lowering of his trembling pelvis, she stops him by grabbing his waist and firmly pushing it up into the air where she holds it until he understands that this is where it must remain. He brings his mouth awkwardly down to peck, flit, pry, at hers, tongue first again, and she stops him, turning her face sharply away. She pushes his head down toward her breasts, holding his head with both her hands so that his mouth is placed right where she intends it — on a breast. She locks his head there, but lifts her nose toward the ceiling to escape the schoolboy sweat trapped in the thick unfashionably short and oily hair. Without looking at him she urgently whispers, "Suck them."

He grabs her waist with his hands and does as he is told with his mouth wide open, tongue barely moving except as caused by the sucking action.

His eyes, wide as Frisbees, remain planted sideways on the shut door. If his hand could reach out far enough to open it in the hope that someone might see — someone who might scold and rage at length, hopefully his mother — he would have done it, as long as it would not have interrupted Mala's frightful insistence. Unnerving to him, really, this encounter with such unusual determination from her. If at his age he could have understood the spectrum of meaning in the word *passion*, he would have at least known that her actions were void of compassion for him. Or for her.

Until he feels her entire body writhing and her hands clutching more intimately (*intimately* is his necessarily flattering interpretation) at his head. The door forgotten quite suddenly, he drops off of one knee and opportunistically angles his crotch in between her widening thighs. He fidgets and fumbles trying to undo the belt of his pants as he drops his other leg and lets his full weight fitfully thump against Mala. She presses up against the hard shaft that seems to have instinctively found its niche even through his smelly, thick, khaki school shorts and her wet panties that she knows very well will not come off. She uses this hardness to arrive at her intended destination long before he could unbuckle his belt.

Instantly her body dissolves into an entirely different mode as if none of the previous had ever happened. She blurts out, "I have to go, it's getting late" — pushes him off of her to the side of the bed, jumps off the bed, pulls her clothing off the floor, and begins to dress. He lies on his stomach, not breathless but airless, with a much deflated face propped in his hand. Confused and hurting, he nevertheless studies her distracted agitation as she fumbles behind her back with the bra snaps. And without notice of him she is gone, as if it were nothing at all.

Clutching her school bag tight against her chest like a shield, Mala hustles to try to beat her father's arrival from work. It's so confusing, she thinks to herself, how one part of her body "sort of" enjoys that kind of thing. But only that part, she insists, wincing from a pain that she can't attribute to any place in particular. She berates herself for knowing well beforehand the inevitability of certain feelings — as if a robbery has taken place inside of her, as if the rest of her body, especially her chest, her heart, has been invaded, tricked, or trapped, or laughed at. And yet, knowing all of this, she is saddened that she would have been so foolish as to have pushed ahead like a steam roller out of control. Young shoots of anger begin to bud inside of her, but not really knowing at what or how to be angry, they wither instantly turning into confusions of frustration, despondency. That tickle, that brief moment of tickle, *especially if she is in control of it*, always seems worth it before it actually happens. It always holds so much promise beforehand — the promise of flight, of fancy, of buoyancy, and elation. But the thrill only ever lasts for that one tiny moment, and then after comes that letdown when she realizes that not a single thing has changed for the better. Instead, quite the opposite seems to happen — she seems to burrow deeper and deeper into a muddy swamp that completely surrounds her, closing in and clutching at her neck. Now, finally on her way home from school, she breaks into silent sobbing. As if she were grieving for someone very dear to her, someone whom she has lost through irreversible death. Not in the least desiring to draw attention to herself from the neighbors, she hastens home swiping at tears that cloud her vision.

The neighborhood children here all attend the same school down the way. They play (and fight) together in the same little cliques in backyards or over on the playground blocks away. Mala's exclusion from these groups persists. Her little sister Asha also experiences the same rejection. It was up here, amongst the neighborhood children, that all this pushing away first started. It wasn't long after the first time that they had showed up at the playground that the other children began congregating in little circles from which it was made very clear that Mala and Asha were unwanted. The other children would stare at them over their shoulders, whispering secrets, turning up their faces in feigned disgust or giggling menacingly. Now Mala runs ahead even faster as she hears their giggles and excited shouts hovering behind the fences. She pulls back to a walk, trying to appear calm, and then overcome by a tangled knot of unidentifiable feelings, she again vaults ahead for brief seconds, trying to escape from herself. Tears ceaselessly well up and then run down salty into her mouth. She again brakes to swift walking to avoid tumbling into potholes or tripping on cracks in the uneven asphalt. Thin clear snot pours down onto her top lip. She daubs her nose mercilessly with the inside of her wrist and abruptly catapults into the blur of an athlete doing the 100-meter dash.

This evening, even though she is aware of the blue-gray tanager that lives amongst the yellow branches of a dwarf coconut tree in a neighboring yard, she doesn't have the spirit to stop and watch it as she often does. Through her wet and puffy eyes she sees it hopping from branch to branch, as if intending to keep up with her pace. Able to muster just enough warm appreciation for this little blue bird to momentarily interrupt her anguish, she looks back at it apologetically as she hurries along. Familiar fences of pink and purple croton, shiny green hibiscus shrubs with red flowers, low bottle-brush trees, and boundary plants blur past her as she again picks up speed, sprinting the last few corners.

Sometimes Mala could swear that if she were to gather enough speed she would certainly be able to take off — flying way up into the air above all these gardens, above the topmost branches of the tallest trees around, and even farther. A frigate bird soaring with other frigates until her entire village below is swallowed up, consumed in an unidentifiable fleck of island adrift like a speck of dust in a vast turquoise seascape.

She unlatches the misshapen wood and wire gate to her father's house, still unable to clearly think through the consequences of not showering off the certain smell of someone else's saliva on her breast, which would no doubt enrage her father beyond sanity, or of scrubbing off such evidence with the unintended result of preparing her body for his nightly visit. It would be best to scrub herself thoroughly, she quickly decides, locking herself in the bathroom for a swift (she must cook his dinner and see that Asha has washed and eaten before he arrives) but merciless shower. She would then rub her body (and Asha's once she too has washed) down with strong smelling camphor and menthol — tiger balm — and they would both complain of flu-like sore muscles.

Sylvia and Wyatt

J. D. Smith

In the last year before school consolidation, before the farm kids were jerked out of the soil and sent to district packing sheds, I taught nine students in a one-roomer, way out on the hard, red, winter wheatfields of northern Montana.

In August I received a list of unfilled positions from Helena, and wrote from California to School District 19, Toole County. "It's a dead-end deal," said Sam Black, the chairman of the school board, when we shook hands on the phone. "One year, then we fold the school and you are dismissed. I won't lie to you. You are the only one who has called about this. We'll take the chance if you will. Five thousand dollars and a place to stay for the school year. Plenty of opportunity for weekend work if you can handle equipment."

There was no bus. The children were delivered to the white frame building by wind-wrinkled mothers smelling of diesel, clabbered milk, and manure, driving stubnosed grain trucks and Oldsmobiles with singing shock absorbers. Through the slumping panes of the teacherage's kitchen window, I could forecast the day's attendance by counting the dust plumes that boiled out of the Sweetgrass Hills and converged on the section-line roads.

For the first weeks, because I wore my hair long and had witnessed the world beyond Great Falls, I was a bug in a mayonnaise jar to the kids, to be viewed through a shell of flat, cautious politeness until it was determined whether I raised welts or spat stinky fluids. The younger ones softened first, handing me their friendship in big wads of giggles. By Columbus Day we were claiming a corner of Rasmussen's wheat field for our school and planting an art-project flag in the dusty stubble. Shortly afterward I was J. D., one of the gang, to most of my students.

But not to Wyatt, who, at age eleven, had read all of Louis L'Amour, and believed it possible to live, and to die, as a gunfighter. Hormones were beginning to gather behind his dinner-plate belt buckle. During history class his entire being focused on fair Sylvia's scant breasts. To Wyatt I was an effete outlander, an agent of change, someone bent on jamming mathematics between him and his bull-riding future.

In the puncture weeds at the perimeter of the pea-gravel parking lot were several ant mounds. Wyatt's courtship of Sylvia consisted of carefully working his freckled hand and lower arm into an ant hill, until he was as warm with a black scurry, then chasing her around the schoolyard yelling "Ant arm man is going to get you! Ant arm man is going to get you!"

During one such episode of cowpoke foreplay, Sylvia went down hard, on both knees, against the lip of the concrete pad that anchored the flag pole.

Restrained tears fogged her glasses. "Damn you, Wyatt. I'll get you." These were strong words from a wispy farm girl who dressed as her grandmother had.

Wyatt booted rocks down the road ahead of us. I was pissed. I told him to cut the crap, to try a little tenderness, that Sylvia was in pain because he had worked an old joke one too many times, and that I didn't like any pain, intentional or accidental, so he'd better come around, settle down, before I called in the big dogs, his folks and Sylvia's, to put the clamps on this foolishness. Wyatt tipped back the bill of his tractor hat, checked the clouds, flashed a coyote grin, and said "Yes, Sir, Mister Smith, Sir." That night a cold front seeped over the Canadian border and covered the ant hills with a foot of snow.

For Christmas I bought each student a harmonica. By Saint Valentine's Day, with Sylvia sitting first chair, we were a one-song band, playing "The Streets of Loredo" to an audience of aquarium guppies. March afternoons were spent in model rocketry, firing chunks of balsa wood and cardboard tubes way, way up into the huge crystal sky, then trudging a mile of frozen prairie for the retrieval. A wind that smelled of crawdads whistled up from the Missouri River breaks in early April. Overnight the snow was gone.

One sunny spring morning, after the red-mud schoolyard had scabbed over enough to permit play, Sylvia and Janet asked if they could take the new canvas bases outside and design a softball diamond. Sure...but mind the windows and the wind.

Each team had a pitcher, a first baseman, and a couple of roving stubblefielders. I was to be both teams' catcher. Wyatt captained one group and chose Sylvia, Janet, and the two first graders for his helpers. Sylvia was unusually aggressive in demanding that her team bat first.

Of course, Wyatt was the leadoff hitter. He punched the first pitch through a hole where the shortstop would've been, a clean single, but the girls knew Wyatt, so as he was scampering up the baseline toward first, Sylvia and Janet were yelling "Take two, Wyatt! Take two!" When he made the turn, going for the double, they changed their chant to "Slide, Wyatt! Slide, Wyatt! Slide Wyatt!" so he slid...headfirst into a busy community of red ants that had recently been covered by second base.

He came up swatting, spitting, and slapping. He was a tough little hombre, but I could see that he was in trouble with this situation, so I hustled him into the four-seater outhouse, jerked off his boots while he tore at the snaps on his shirt, and helped him brush the cooties off his back and out of his hair. I left as he fought with his belt buckle. Sylvia sat smiling in the swing.

A month later the job ended. On the last day of school, as I was boxing the artifacts of my teaching career, I looked into the schoolyard and saw Wyatt and Sylvia holding hands while they waited for their rides home.

Nine Now

Kirsten Smith

This must be fun for you,
doing all these grown-up things,
I say to my son, with his
blood blisters and his ballpark scabs
and his eyes just like mine.
Sure, he says and I can see
that, even though he is only nine now,
he is close to growing past me,
past hand-holding and scallywagging
and into the double digits of his life.
Soon he will start his surge
towards the grim wonder of adolescence,
littered with its newfound *shits* and *damns*, its Carries
and its Erins, their tongues nestling next to his.
And I will grow older as well, there will be nights

when I am too stunned with sitcoms and specials
to notice the driveway blooming with girls,
Kentucky cuties and Kansas City babes,
Scandinavian maids and Irish lasses,
all of them having traveled the tattered roadway
to reach my son, this miracle of *maybes* and *Sure, Moms*.
They will have come to touch the skin I made in a night
    with his father,
the mouth that spouts slang I've never heard before,
the lashes that hum down over the eyes.
The nines and tens of his life will be kissed goodbye
by the glossy mouths of learner's permits and twelve
    packs,
his lips resting on the collarbone of boyhood,
fingers fumbling at the clasp of his new guy world.

My Sister's Body

Kirsten Smith

I have been living in my sister's room
for so long,
I begin to think that
her body is mine.
The long torso,
the breasts lodged high
like tea cakes
on her powdery skin.
In our room
I watch my sister dash around,
her lips like bruised plums
as she waits for Danny
to gun up to the house.
With no mirror to see
my burning, twelve-year-old self,
I look at her
and memorize everything.
So when the time comes,
and the boy's eye glitters like a crime,
I will know what to do.
I will peel off my crushed velvet shell
and stand before him
tall and beautiful
and so white
he can barely breathe.

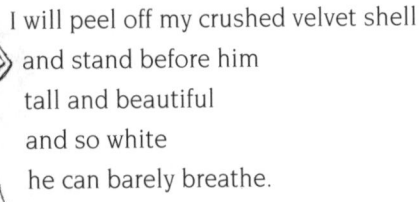

129

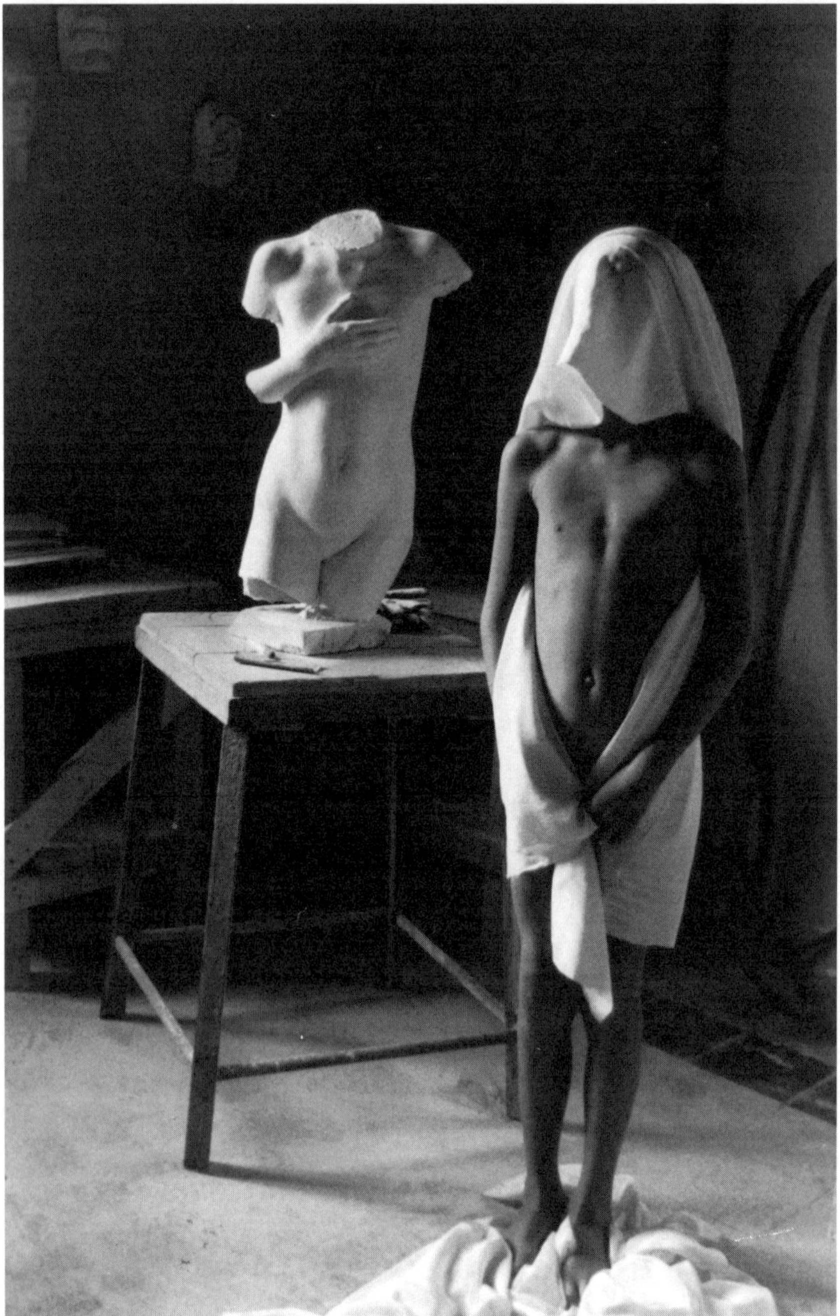

Photos by Marly Stone

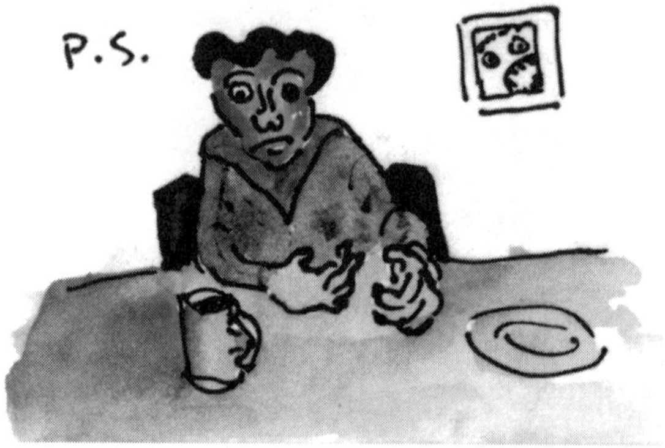
P.S.

Guide to Parenting: Lessons I, II, III

Rachel Hoffman

I: MISS AMERICA

Mother says, "What ever happened to your dream of being Miss America?"

I laugh. I say, "I grew up."

"Remember?" mother says. "We cried every time Miss America took her first steps down the runway."

I was thirteen, and mother enrolled me for training at Patricia Lewis Charm Academy. I was going to be Miss America. Every Saturday, for two months, I joined nine other adolescent Miss America hopefuls at the Patricia Lewis Charm Academy.

For eight Saturdays I dressed by the point system. Fashion co-ordination points began with the accessories. If I chose shoes and a bag of different colors, then the shoes and bag had to be of the same material. On the other hand, my shoes and bag could be of different materials as long as they were all the same color. Unless patent leather was involved. Then both bag and shoes had to be the same color no matter what. My shoes had to be darker than the hem of my dress unless I chose to wear no jewelry. If I wore no jewelry, my shoes could in fact be lighter than the hem of my dress and, thus, count as decorative points. If I wanted to wear earrings and a necklace at the same time, I would not wear a hat. If, by some odd chance I did wish to wear a hat, then a necklace would be preferable to earrings. Unless I was wearing gloves and then I would have to wear a hat. If I were to wear a hat, I'd have to select a complementary belt and any decision regarding earrings, then, would be out of my hands.

"Did you know," the Charm Instructor asked, "that when a lady sits and folds her hands in her lap, her hands are placed one inside the other, palms-up, fingers relaxed and bent slightly to display the lady's perfectly manicured fingernails."

"And," the Charm Instructor said, "there is a correct way for a lady to smile."

"A lady," she said, "smiles only with her mouth and not with her eyes or eyebrows."

"What is more," she said, "Never, ever, under any circumstances does a lady, when she smiles, reveal her gums."

The Charm Instructor demonstrated.

"When a lady enters a room," the Charm Instructor said, smiling her smile without revealing her gums, "she hands the doorknob from hand to hand behind her back so not to have to turn her back to the people in the room, and she unbuttons her coat with one hand only and from bottom to top adding lilt and lift to her entire appearance."

One Saturday halfway into the training, the charm class learned makeup. The Charm Instructor began by applying depilatory to a Hispanic girl's upper lip and pancake makeup to another girl's acne.

My turn came. The Charm Instructor said my mouth was too full, my hair was too long and straight, the bridge of my nose was freckled and too broad, and my eyebrows were too bushy.

The Charm Instructor said she was no plastic surgeon, but she would do what she could. She plucked out my eyebrows. All of them. She said, "Don't worry, dear, they'll grow back soon enough," and she wiped away the blood.

The Charm Instructor penciled correct eyebrows onto my forehead. She rolled the eyebrow pencil point across her tongue and applied moist brown lines to my forehead. She pinched the bridge of my nose, stood back, and handed me a mirror.

I took the mirror. I smiled a gumless smile at the Charm Instructor and thanked her, but I knew I couldn't look into the mirror and see the ugly girl with the full mouth, the broad nose, and no eyebrows.

I could have said, "No. Stop."

Instead I thanked her.

"No. Stop," is not something the Charm Instructor taught me to say.

The pancake-makeup-girl's acne is inflamed. The Hispanic girl has the beginnings of mustache growth. My eyebrows are gone.

Full orchestra.

Bert Parks steps from behind the red velvet drapes and up to the microphone. He says, "Ladies and Gentlemen. We now begin the talent portion of our competition. It is my distinct pleasure to introduce the contestant from one of our oldest and most problematic states, the State of Adolescence, Miss Suzy Harvey, who will, for the next several years of her anguished youth, be performing a series of unnatural acts…"

I can set a formal table. I know how to curtsey to the floor for the Queen of England. I can enter a room and smile without revealing my gums.

Parents were seated.

Every girl took her walk down the runway.

Mother cried for her Miss America.

II: PAULA

Paula and I were fourteen.

I knew how to curtsey for the Queen of England and smile without revealing my gums. I got A's in school, but Paula knew about physiology. Paula understood Jim Morrison when he sang "Break On Through to the Other Side."

Paula's mom introduced me to Mop and Glow, Good Seasons Salad Dressing Mix, Coca Cola in six-packs, and Cadillacs. The family was Republican, and I watched Richard Millhouse Nixon get elected President on the color television at Paula's house.

At Christmas, Paula's dad unboxed the pink-flocked aluminum pine tree in the garage. He screwed pink evergreen branches into a pink pipe stem and wrapped pink cotton batting snow around the three-pronged base. Paula and I hung glass balls.

There was always a gift tagged "Suzy." I was neither Christian nor Republican, but Paula's mother thought I was a good influence on Paula. Jewish people know how to make money.

The nights I slept over, Paula and I set the alarm clock for one AM We stuffed Paula's big four-poster, white lace canopied bed with clothes and pillows. Then Paula and I climbed out Paula's bedroom window, ran around the corner, and met up with Paula's nineteen-year-old boyfriend. Gary.

Gary had a broken front tooth. Gary wore leather bell-bottoms with fringes up the sides. Gary played the tambourine and drove a black van with flames painted on the fender.

One night Paula's nineteen-year-old boyfriend brought along a friend for me. Rob.

Paula and Gary and Rob and I went to Gary's apartment.

An American flag hung from the ceiling. Behind the flag was a black light, and the light filtered through the white parts of the flag so stripes fell across the Jimi Hendrix posters.

Paula took a drag off a joint. She said, "Excuse me while I kiss the sky."

ಅಗಿ

When I was seven years old, mother sat me down and read me an entire book on human reproduction. The book used words like fallopian tube and spermatozoa and ejaculation.

A week after she read me the book, I came home from Beethoven Street Elementary School and said, "Mommy, what does fuck mean?"

I spent the rest of the day in my room.

~~~

Rob and I used the fold-up camp cot in a corner of the room.

I don't know how Rob managed what he managed to do on that camp cot, but I hadn't learned to say "No, Stop," and he managed.

There was no sheet. No pillow. No blanket. Rob's pants were unzipped and he was on top of me. One of Rob's hands held my wrists above my head. He called me Babe.

At three AM Rob took Gary's keys and drove Paula and me to Dunkin' Donuts.

Gary didn't come along. Gary wouldn't wake up.

Dunkin' Donuts at three AM The fluorescent lights vibrated green.

Paula and I had Homeroom at eight, so Rob dropped us around the corner from Paula's bedroom window.

Rob said to me, "Hey, babe. I'll call you."

III: NEW SHOES

"Our last pair," the department store shoe salesman says.

The shoe box is wedged under the salesman's left arm and he's reaching around, down past the shoe box into his suit pockets.

"Size nine," the salesman says.

I say, "Is that what the foot measure said? Size nine?"

"The shoes run large," the salesman says.

I say, "But I wear a ten."

The salesman's left hand clutches a shoe horn. His right hand holds the chopped-off, ankle-high footends of two stockings.

"I'm telling you lady," the salesman says. He shakes the stocking feet at me. "The shoes run large."

~~~

My first bra was too small, too.

I was twelve. I wore braces and orthopedic oxfords. I was tall. I slouched and tripped often.

And I had to carry a boxed bra, size 26AAA, and stand with grown men and women in the Merchandise Return Line at the Emporium.

"Every girl in my class except me wears a bra."

I cried for three hours before I could say that to mother.

Mother said, "So that's what all the fuss is about."

A week later mother came home with a training bra. Size 26AAA.

I took the bra into the bathroom and locked the door.

I tried, but I couldn't make the bra close around me. I arched and twisted to hook the bra in back. I put it around my waist and I could get it hooked, but then I couldn't get it up past the bottom of my rib cage and put my arms through the straps at the same time.

I took one end of the bra in each hand and straightened my arms outward to stretch the thing bigger.

"Open up, Suzy," mother said. "What are you doing in there?"

I unlocked the door.

"My, my," mother said. "I guess we need a larger size. Did you keep the box?"

I look at the shoe salesman, box of shoes still wedged under his arm. I say, "When you chop off the feet at the ankles, where do the rest of the stockings go?"

"Pardon me?" the shoe salesman says.

I point at the chopped-off stocking feet in the salesman's right hand and say, "What do you do with the leg part of the stockings?"

The shoe salesman looks at the stocking feet. Then he looks at me. "I don't chop off the feet, lady. They come this way. In a big, brown, corrugated cardboard box. In back."

He says, "Do we want to try on the shoes now?" He shakes the stocking feet at me.

I look at the stocking feet. I look at the shoe salesman. I pull on my size ten top-stitched, red cowgirl boots. I stand up and stretch to a good four inches taller than the shoe salesman. I twist my long straight hair over my shoulder. I smile big and reveal my gums.

"Thank you," I say. "No."

What is a Normal Family and Childhood?

Stephanie Coontz

Most debates over whether contemporary parents are neglecting their children or investing unprecedented amounts of energy and resources in them seem to me to miss the point. The two trends not only coexist but often feed each other. Both are inextricably linked to a definition of good parenting that is a comparatively recent historical invention — and not an unequivocal improvement over the past.

The notion that the more parental time, attention, and intensity the better — with its corollary assumption that love, discipline, self-esteem, and values are fostered almost exclusively at home, through the bonding of parent and child — turns some families into pressure cookers and offers others no criteria for differentiating between neglect and the mistakes or exasperations that have always been a part of family life, and always will be. All too often, this notion also prevents us from seeking or offering support beyond the family.

Such a value system can be profoundly antisocial. For every child we rear who says to a neighbor down the block, "You can't tell me what to do; you're not my mom," we produce an adult who says, "I don't care what happens to them; they're not *my* children." And even within such tight-knit families, these values have a built-in tendency to self-destruct. The failure of family life to live up to romanticized ideals can lead people to abandon family commitments altogether in their search for fulfillment; unrealistic expectations turn easily to rage.

Few societies in history have shared our insistence on the unique role of the nuclear family, especially mothers, in meeting all their children's needs and shaping their personalities. Yet despite years of studying the ways that other cultures and historical periods have raised well-adjusted children and socially responsible adults, without our Ozzie and Harriet expectations of the perfect parent, I only realized how limited, not to mention exhausting, were modern American standards of good parenting when I spent some time with Hawaiian-Filipino friends on the island of Lanai. My child was still in diapers, and I greatly appreciated the fact that nearly every community function, from weddings to New Year's Eve parties, was open to children. I could sit and socialize and keep an eye on my toddler, and I assumed that was what all the other parents were doing. Soon, however, I noticed that I was the only person jumping up to change a diaper, pick my son up when he fell, wipe his nose, dry his eyes, or ply him with goodies. Belatedly, I realized why: the other parents were not keeping an eye on their kids. Instead, each adult kept an eye on the floor around his or her chair. Any child who moved into that section of the floor and needed disciplining, feeding, comforting, or changing was promptly accommodated; no parent felt compelled to check that his or her *own* child was being similarly cared for.

When such generalized responsibility for children exists, kids may learn *more* self-esteem, confidence, and social trust than when they must depend for care and nurture only on the love of their "own" parents. Talcott Parsons and other sociologists of the 1950s claimed that the small, intense nuclear family was best suited to childraising in modern industrial society, and the Moynihan Report of the 1960s argued that lack of a tight nuclear family with a strong father figure created weak egos among black Americans. But Richard Sennett found in nineteenth-century Chicago that it was the small nuclear families of the white middle class who were least able to operate successfully in the industrial economy and most likely to produce weak egos. Among the Mbuti pygmies, every three-year-old enters the *bopi*, a private world of the children in which they live, play, perform sacred rituals such as lighting the purification fires for adult hunters, and from which they exclude adults for the bulk of the day. One of their first lessons here is the overwhelming importance of cooperation and equality in pygmy life but "the relative unimportance of gender and biological kinship."

I am not suggesting that we should turn modern child care centers into *bopi*, nor would I argue that some specific alternative to the nuclear family should become our new cultural ideal. While some people long for the solidarity and mutual aid of extended families, for example, we also know that such families sometimes exercise brutal repression over women and children. The point is that there is no magic form or formula that justifies cutting and pasting families to make them conform to a single pattern.

Of *course* children need continuity and nurture in their lives, but there are many ways of providing that. A wide variety of family forms and childrearing arrangements have worked (and not worked) in different historical and cultural settings. While modern Americans tend to think that a girl needs an especially close relationship to her mother and a boy to his father, other societies create well-adjusted children in different ways. Among the Cheyenne, a girl is expected to have strained, even hostile, relations with her mother and to go to her aunt for comfort and guidance. In the Trobriand Islands, a man has much closer relations with his sister's sons than with his own; his biological sons are counted as part of his wife's family, not his own.

The Zinacantecos of southern Mexico lack a word differentiating parents and children from other social groupings; instead, they identify the basic unit of social and personal responsibility as a "house." In medieval Europe and colonial America, as well as in many contemporary West African societies, fosterage, child exchange, and adoption have been as central to childrearing as have actual blood ties. In pre-industrial Europe, "contracts of brotherhood" and other arrangements linked domestic groups into "tacit communities" of both extended families and non-kin. In Hawaii, to offer a child as a "hanai" adoption to a childless relative or friend has historically been an act of love, not abandonment. In the Caribbean, the co-parenting of children by unrelated individuals or couples creates enduring ties beyond the nuclear family, while godparent or co-madre and co-padre relations function in the same way in many other cultures. Failure to understand that these family forms are as meaningful to the people who live in them as our own families are to us leads to tragic misunderstandings. In West Africa, fostering a child out is a way of building social trust and providing the child with new resources and educational experience; the natal family does not relinquish its claim or commitment to the child. But when West Africans engage in this practice in England, they often find that English couples sue for permanent custody and English judges consider them to have abandoned their children.

For some commentators, "the history of childhood is a nightmare from which we have only recently begun to awaken." But history does not lend itself to sweeping unilineal generalizations. Abandonment, for example, was very widespread in the Middle Ages. Indeed, Jean-Jacques Rousseau, the great proponent of sentimental love and female domesticity, put all five of his own infants in a foundling hospital. Yet in many cases, "abandoned" children were followed by their families, often too poverty-stricken to raise them, and reclaimed in later life. Colonial Americans also sanctioned the beating and whipping of children as a legitimate form of punishment. Yet historian John Demos argues that there was no pattern of systematic, severe, and escalating abuse such as we see in so many modern child-battering cases. Today we are shocked by the way Colonial Americans tried to inspire fear in their children. The clergyman Cotton Mather, for example, described taking his young daughter into his study and explaining that when he died, which might be very soon, she must remember all he had taught her about combating "the sinful and woeful conditions of her nature." After the eighteenth century, by contrast, there was a growing desire to protect children from fear, but parents attempted to instill *guilt* in its place. One of Louisa May Alcott's vignettes about how to deal with a recalcitrant child involved having the naughty boy hit the *grownup* with a ruler: as this was fiction, the child was immediately overcome with "a passion of love, and shame, and penitence." Some parents claimed to accomplish the same results in real life. The minister Francis Wayland, for example, described how he avoided using physical punishment by isolating his stubborn fifteen-month-old child for thirty-one hours (going into the room periodically to see if he would do as bidden), until the boy not only submitted but also "repeatedly kissed me." In fact, reported the delighted father, he would now kiss anyone he was asked to, "so full of love was he to all the family." Historian Jan Lewis, however, argues that such childrearing practices produced not love but obsequiousness.

Toward the end of the nineteenth century, there developed what historian Viviana Zeliger calls a "sacralization" of childhood in America. This helped spur the abolition of child labor and made it unacceptable to value children for their economic contributions to the family. While most modern Americans find older calculative attitudes toward children's economic worth repulsive, it is by no means clear that "altruistic" parenting produces better childhood experiences. As historian E.P. Thompson comments: "feeling may be more, rather than less, tender or intense *because* relations are 'economic' and critical to mutual survival." The fact that children have less to offer the middle-class family in modern America and that there are few economic reinforcements of parent-child interactions means there are few supports to shore up the bonds of "love."

The degree of instrumental or affective feeling that seems to prevail in a family predicts very little about actual relationships. Louise Tilley has demonstrated through careful individual histories that family strategies based on economic calculation and even child-sacrificing work patterns could be extremely loving *or* extremely brutal; conversely, families who value love and altruism often experience bitter disillusion and violence. There are also class and cultural components to childrearing values that lead easily to misunderstanding. Working-class and peasant families, for example, have historically tended to disguise individual, personal feelings in "tough talk," partly in order to ensure that family ties do not threaten larger social solidarities; middle-class families have tended to wrap material interests and status considerations in an individualized, voluntaristic, and sentimental language. To assume that one familial language reveals more "pure" or "admirable" sentiments toward children is very naive.

If parental, class, and cultural ideas about childrearing have varied enormously over time, so have the pronouncements of "experts" about what parents must and must not do. In the eighteenth and early nineteenth centuries, it was thought that children should be taught academic subjects at a very early age; in 1830, a substantial portion of children under the age of four were enrolled in school. By the mid-nineteenth century, however, expert consensus held that early schooling caused children to burn out or even become stupid in later years.

In the early twentieth century, experts counseled parents against "fussing" over infants or picking them up when they cried, and advocated rigid feeding and sleeping schedules. "The rule that parents should not play with the baby may seem hard," cautioned one government pamphlet, "but it is without doubt a safe one." During the same period, however, many teens and preteens, such as urban newsboys and peddlers, were granted a freedom from supervision that makes many modern latchkey children look positively cosseted.

By the 1940s and 1950s, a more flexible, affectionate approach to babies was in vogue, although this was also the period when breastfeeding was judged inferior to "scientific" artificial feeding. Permissive attitudes toward babies, moreover, coexisted with far tighter reins on adolescents. While some authors offer 1950s mothering as a model for good parenting, arguing that since the 1960s, women's search for fulfillment outside the family has loosened family ties and created insecure, narcissistic personalities, others suggest that narcissism is rooted in the 1950s family model itself, which "isolates mothers from adult companionship, denies their needs for meaningful work, and enforces their exclusive responsibility for childrearing."

Changes in childrearing values and parental behaviors are seldom a result of people suddenly becoming nicer or meaner, smarter or more irresponsible. They reflect realignments in the way families articulate with larger social, economic, and political institutions, as well as changes in environmental demands on adults and children. Often these realignments involve painful personal transitions; sometimes they simply do not work. But when the distribution of income, jobs, age groups, and gender roles is changing as rapidly as it is today, it is not helpful to exhort families to go back to a "traditional" parenting ideal that developed in a totally different socioeconomic climate and that never did work as well or for as many people as the sitcom reruns might lead one to believe.

All this is not to say that we can't make value judgments about what works in childraising and what doesn't. But the historical evidence demonstrates that two criteria are much more significant than the structure of the family or its childcare arrangements. First, families raise children most successfully when societies adapt their social institutions to changing work and living patterns, instead of demanding that parents single-handedly hold at bay all the changes that may be going on. Second, the best predictor of a family's ability to raise flexible and competent children, and to respond successfully to stress, is not its internal form or values but its access to social support networks beyond the family.

What this means for us today is that the closest thing to a perfect parent is one who realizes there's no such thing. We all need support systems and social institutions to help us build on our strengths, compensate for our weaknesses, and teach our children to act as members of a community that is much larger than their own nuclear family, and just as worthy of commitment and respect.

Biographies

David Axelrod is the author of a collection of poems, *Jerusalem of Grass* (Ahsahta), and a limited edition of the long poem excerpted here. New work has appeared recently or is forthcoming in *The Webster Review*, *Green Mountains Review*, *Chiron Review*, *Duckabush Journal*. He is currently completing a new collection of poems, *Imperfect Forms*.

Sherman Alexie, a Spokane/Coeur d'Alene Indian, is the author of *First Indian on the Moon*, a book of poems from Hanging Loose Press, and *The Lone Ranger and Tonto Fistfight in Heaven* (the paperback will be published in September, 1994 by HarperCollins). His upcoming books include a limited edition of poems from Limberlost Press late in 1994 and a novel, *Coyote Springs*, in 1995 from Grove Atlantic. James is on the honor role at Reardon Junior High School and runs the mile in track.

Stephanie Coontz is a member of the faculty in history at Evergreen State College in Olympia, Washington. Her most recent book, from which her essay is adapted, is *The Way We Never Were: American Families and the Nostalgia Trap*. Her previous work, *The Social Origins of Private Life: A History of American Families, 1600–1900*, was awarded the Washington Governor's Writers Award.

Stephanie has testified about her research before The House Select Committee on Children, Youth, and Families in Washington, D.C. In addition to academic journals, she has written for a wide range of national publications, including *The New York Times*, *Harper's*, *The Washington Post*, and *Elle*. She has lectured throughout Europe and the United States and been featured in several documentaries on family issues and gender relations.

Brian Doyle is the editor of *Portland Magazine* at the University of Portland. His essays and stories have appeared in *The American Scholar*, *Commonweal*, and *Reader's Digest*, among other publications. Recently his wife told him they were going to have another child. He is thrilled and afraid. He wishes he could protect his children from evil. It angers him that he cannot. He continues to maintain that life is a miracle and that a conversation with a child is an encounter with God. His daughter Lily told him the other day that she would like to wear sunshine today.

Juan Armando Epple's story was written in Spanish and translated by Ken Inness as a class project for a seminar on Literary Translation. "In their innocent play they [two children] are repeating the social and ideological patterns of the adult world, particularly the rigid working-class sex roles still prevailing in the Latin American societies, and to a certain extent, even here in the U.S. I think that Ken was able to render a very good translation, considering the stylistic problems posed by a story that uses primarily the subjunctive mode to convey the Spanish notion of uncertainty."

Juan received his Licenciatura from the Austral University of Chile and his master's and Ph.D. from Harvard University. He has edited several anthologies of short fiction, including *Cruzando la Cordillera*, *Brevisima relación del cuento breve de Chile*, and *Brevisima relación: Antologia del micro-cuento hispanoamericano*, as well as numerous articles on Latin American and Chicano literature. A short story writer, some of his stories have appeared in *Chilean Writers in Exile* (The Crossing Press, 1986), and *Cuentos hispanos de los Estados Unidos* (Arte Público Press, 1993). He teaches Spanish American and Chicano literature at the University of Oregon.

Mikal Gilmore, a contributing editor for *Rolling Stone*, was working on one of his first assignments for that magazine when he learned his elder brother, Gary, convicted of murdering two men in Utah, was campaigning to have his life ended by firing squad. His book, *Shot in the Heart*, relates the events that led to and followed his brother's execution.

Rachel Hoffman lives in Portland, Oregon. She is a recipient of a 1993 Oregon Institute of Literary Arts Fiction Prize for a novel-in-progress.

Miles Inada, whose illustrations grace these pages, is a giant squid from Ashland with a B.A. in English from Yale University and a B.F.A. in painting from the University of Oregon. He currently lives deep within the Willamette River with his lovely wife, Julie.

Shani Mootoo is an Irish-born, Indo-Trinidadian writer, visual artist, and videomaker now living in Vancouver, British Columbia. Her current work addresses issues of race, gender, sexuality and identity, and challenges dominant stereotypes of the role and place of women, particularly South Asian women. Her visual art has been shown in exhibitions locally and internationally. In the last two years she has written and directed four successful videos, including *English Lesson* (1992) and *The Wild Woman in the Woods* (1993). In addition, her writing has been published in *Fuse* magazine, *Absinthe*, and in several Gallerie Women Artists' Monographs. Her first book of short fiction, *Out On Main Street*, was published by Press Gang Publishers, Vancouver, B.C.

Ann Rule. "Since 1965, I have worked full-time as an author and lecturer. I have published in national magazines such as: *Cosmopolitan*, *Redbook*, *True Detective*, *Official Detective*, and newspapers such as the *Chicago Tribune* and the *Seattle Times*. I have published nine books: *The Stranger Beside Me*, *Possession*, *Lust Killer*, *The Want-Ad Killer*, *The I-5 Killer*, *Beautiful Seattle*, *Small Sacrifices*, *If You Really Loved Me* and *Everything She Ever Wanted*.

"All of my books are required reading for criminal justice and psychology classes in many universities in America. I am a certified instructor for police, parole, and probation officers in Oregon, Texas, Idaho, Virginia, California, and for the National Institute of Corrections in the U.S. Justice Department. I often speak to women's groups on how they may protect themselves from violent crime, and help support, financially and emotionally, a victims' support group: Families and Friends of Victims of Violent Crimes and Missing Persons. I'm also involved with Child Help, an organization which provides help to any child who needs it."

Joe Sacco's *Palestine* is a nine-issue series currently being published by Fantagraphics Books. It is based on a two-month visit he made to Jerusalem and the Occupied Territories in the winter of 1991–1992. His previous comic book series was entitled *Yahoo*. Joe has a degree in journalism from the University of Oregon and resides in Portland.

Cyan Sichel made the art that graces this *Left Bank*'s cover last year when she was nine years-old. It was created at Open Palm Studio in Portland, Oregon. This is one of the places where Cyan explores art and where she is joined by many special young artists who support, encourage, and inspire each other in the journey of creativity. Sixty-seven artists attend sessions where they use a wide variety of art media, tools, and techniques to make art. Started three years ago by Deborah Kalapsa, Open Palm Studio is dedicated to nurturing the artist that exists in us all.

J.D. Smith is an over-fifty, hungry writer/househusband with two children twenty-one years apart. He spends the daylight hours cooking noodles and designing an adhesive bandage compatible with nearly any external wound that can by inflicted by a two-year-old son.

Kirsten Smith has poems forthcoming in *Prairie Schooner*, *The Massachusetts Review*, *Witness*, *Quarterly West*, *Amelia*, *Spoon River Quarterly*, *The Berkeley Poetry Review* and *Poet Lore*. She works for Projekt Records in Los Angeles and her manuscript of poems, *Kissing Beside the Kill*, is currently in circulation.

Matthew Stadler is the author of *Landscape: Memory* and *The Dissolution of Nicholas Dee*. His story is from his forthcoming novel, *The Sex Offender*, to be published by HarperCollins in September, 1994. He won a Guggenheim Fellowship in 1992.

Neal Stephenson issues from a clan of rootless, itinerant hard-science and engineering professors (mostly Pac-10, Big 10, and Big 8 with the occasional wild strain of Ivy). He began his higher education as a physics major, then switched to geography when it appeared that this would enable him to scam more free time on his university's mainframe computer. When he graduated and discovered, to his perplexity, that there were no jobs for inexperienced physicist-geographers, he began to look into alternative pursuits such as working on cars, unimaginably stupid agricultural labor, and writing novels. His first novel, *The Big U*, was published in 1984 and vanished without a trace. His second novel, *Zodiac: the Eco-thriller*, came out in 1988 and quickly developed a cult following among water-pollution-control engineers. It was also enjoyed, though rarely bought, by many radical environmentalists. *Snow Crash* was written in the years 1988 through 1991 as the author listened to a great deal of loud, relentless, depressing music.

Neal resides in a comfortable home in the western hemisphere and spends all of his time trying to retrofit an office into its generally dark, unlevel, and asbestos-laden basement so that he can attempt to write more novels. Despite the tremendous amounts of time he devotes to writing, playing with computers, listening to speed metal, Rollerblading, and pounding nails, he is a flawless husband, parent, neighbor, and all-around human being.

Marly Stone, a photographer, sculptor, and painter, has her work in many collections including the Museum of Modern Art in New York, the Biblioteque Nationale in Paris, and the Portland Art Museum in Portland, Oregon. She has had over a dozen one-woman exhibitions including the Museum of Modern Art, Oxford, England, the H.F. Manes Gallery in New York City, and the Biota Gallery in Los Angeles.

Sallie Tisdale's newest book, Talk Dirty To Me: An Intimate Philosophy of Sex will be published by Doubleday in November, 1994. She lives in Oregon.

Virginia Euwer Wolff's novel, Make Lemonade (Henry Holt, 1993), won the Bank Street Child Study Book Award and the Society of Children's Book Publishers & Illustrator's Golden Kite, and was selected as Top of the List by Booklist. Her earlier prize-winning books for young readers are The Mozart Season and Probably Still Nick Swansen.

Virginia says, "It seems to me that if we really cared about kids, all of us would boycott all products sold by sponsors of television that glorify violence and exploit sexuality-as-loveless-conquest. And we would make sure that art and music have a permanent place in all of our schools, accessible to all of our children. I doubt that we'll ever come together enough as a society to do that."

RICOCHET RIVER

ROBIN CODY weaves powerful threads of time, place, and character into a complex coming-of-age story set in the sixties, in the NW — or anytime, anywhere.

Wade is the local sports hero and Lorna's boyfriend. Lorna knows there's no future in Calamus. Not for a bright girl like her. Not for Wade. And definately not for Jesse, the Indian kid who plays by his own rules.

ISBN 0-936085-27-4, $11.95 + $2.50 s/h, or request catalog from:

Blue Heron Publishing, 24450 NW Hansen, Hillsboro, OR 97124. Credit card orders:

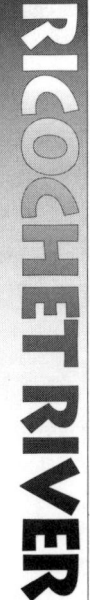

Writing Across Cultures
A Handbook on Writing Poetry & Lyrical Prose
Edna Kovacs

"...makes the point quite clear: poetry, communication, and the exchange of language are universal human capabilities...which traverse borders, boudaries, nations, and colors." — Luis Rodriquez, author of Always Running: La Vida Loca, Gang Days in LA

From African Drum Song to Blues, Ghazal to Haiku, Villanelle to the Zoo, this playful book stimulates the writing of poetry and lyrical prose. Samples from Le Guin, Lorca, Roethke, Basho, Piercy, W.C. Williams, and many others — with student work, as well.

$11.95 + $2.50 s/h, 6 x 9, 186 pages, ISBN 0-986085-25-8. Blue Heron Publishing, 24450 NW Hansen Rd, Hillsboro OR 97124, or by credit card at 800/858-9055.

GLIMMER TRAIN'S SHORT-STORY AWARD FOR NEW WRITERS

- 1,200–7,500 word limit.
- Held twice yearly and open to any writer whose fiction hasn't appeared in a nationally distributed publication with a circulation over 5,000.
- $10 reading fee (covers up to two stories sent together in the same envelope).
- Entries must be postmarked during the months of February/March or August/September.
- First page of story to include name, address, phone.
- Please staple your story, rather than using a paper clip.
- "Short-Story Award for New Writers" should be written on the outside of your envelope.

- Winner receives $1,200 and publication in *Glimmer Train Stories*.
- First/second runners-up receive $500/$300, respectively, and honorable mention.
- Winners notified by July 1 (for Feb./March entrants) and Jan. 1 (for Aug./Sept. entrants).
- Please do not send a SASE, as materials will not be returned.
- We cannot acknowledge receipt or provide status of any particular manuscript.
- All applicants receive a copy of the issue in which winning entry is published and runners-up announced.

GLIMMER TRAIN

stories stories stories stories stories

812 SW Washington Street, Suite 1205, Portland, Oregon 97205 USA
Co-Presidents Susan Burmeister-Brown, Linda Davies   Facsimile 503/221-0837

Free Catalog
Bargain Books

Save up to 80% on recent overstocks, remainders, imports and reprints from all major publishers—America's biggest bargain book selection.

Choose from yesterday's best sellers to titles you never knew existed. Over 40 subject areas: Biography, History, Fiction, Politics, the Arts, Gardening, Cooking and more—with more books by mail at lower prices than you'll find anywhere else.

- **Save up to 80%. Books as low as $1.95, $2.95, $3.95**
- **Thousands of titles in each catalog issue**
- **Over 40 subject areas**
- **48-hour shipment, and a moneyback guarantee**

Send me your FREE Catalog of Bargain Books.

Name
Address
City
State   Zip

HAMILTON Box 15-469
Falls Village, CT 06031

CALYX LITERATURE BY WOMEN

▲ THE VIOLET SHYNESS OF THEIR EYES: NOTES FROM NEPAL
by Barbara J. Scot

A woman's physical and spiritual journey.

Barbara Scot gives us the Nepal she saw, touched, visited with a feminist's respect for difference....Hers is a tale of sharing, and we are privileged to see through her eyes, understand through her exquisite sensibility.
— Margaret Randall

Women's Studies, 286 pages, bw photos, $12.95 paper, $22.95 cloth

---

Finalist, 1993 WESTAF Book Awards!

▲ RAISING THE TENTS
by Frances Payne Adler

Moving poetry that portrays a woman's journey out of silence. A Jewish pulse with feminist vision and wise humor. A woman "raising the tents" so that we can see what has not been visible, hear what has not been spoken, probing the crevices of memory... cherishing all peoples.
— Bettina Aptheker

Poetry, 96 pages, $9.95 paper, $19.95 cloth

▲ OPEN HEART
by Judith Mickel Sornberger

An elegant collection of poetry rooted in a woman's relationships with family, ancestors, and the world. A testimony to the strength and immortality of the human spirit. What an openness to life and its teachings, what an openness to the being of others so that somehow they come pulsingly alive; what deep-won comprehension over years has gone into creating these poems.
— Tillie Olsen

Poetry, 128 pages, $9.95 paper, $19.95 cloth

CALYX Books are available to the trade from Consortium Book Sales & Distribution, Inc., and from other wholesalers and small press distributors.

▲ CALYX, Inc. ▲ P.O. BOX B ▲ CORVALLIS, OR 97339•0539
▲ (503) 753•9384 ▲ Fax (503) 753•0515 ▲

ZYZZYVA

puts West Coast writers on the map

We only publish writers who live in AK, CA, HI, OR, or WA, because publishing is dominated by the East, and the talent in our neighborhood deserves a flagship journal.

Kathy Acker Opal Palmer Adisa Etel Adnan Francisco X. Alarcón Christopher Alexander Peter Alexander Sherman Alexie Paula Gunn Allen Isabel Allende Cathyrn Alpert Michael Amnasan Don Asher Joe Banks Bill Barich Dick Barnes David Barth Ramón C. Bautista Marvin Bell Michael S. Bell Dodie Bellamy Steve Benson Bill Berkson Lucia Berlin Dan Bern Alan Bernheimer Lisa Bernstein Gina Berriault Duane BigEagle Charles Boccadoro Chana Bloch Bill Bradd Kris Brandenburger James M. Brantingham Leo Braudy Kate Braverman Summer Brenner Peter Brett James Broughton Peter Browning Deborah Bruner Charles Bukowski Douglas Bullis Lorna Dee Cervantes Marilyn Chandler Neeli Cherkovski Marilyn Chin Eric Chock Thomas Christensen Tom Clark Anthony Clarvoe Michelle T. Clinton Benjamin E. Colby Wanda Coleman Gillian Conoley Dennis Cooper Alfred Coppel Peter Coyote Alev Lytle Croutier Beverly Dahlen John Daniel Michael Davidson Jean Day Denise Dee Gene Dennis W.S. Di Piero Craig L. Diaz William Dickey Sharon Doubiago Alan Dundes Katherine Dunn Stephen Emerson George Evans Lawrence Ferlinghetti M.F.K. Fisher Claudia Stillman Franks Lynn Freed Judith Freeman Joshua Freiwald Benjamin Friedlander Gloria Frym Blair Fuller G.G. Gach Tess Gallagher Abram George Amy Gerstler Martha Gies Barry Gifford Molly Giles Rene Girard Robert Glück Charles Shelby Goerlitz Rocky Gómez Guillermo Gómez-Peña Jill Gonet Charles Goodrich Philip Kan Gotanda Judy Grahn Samuel Green Richard Grossinger Thom Gunn John Haines Sam Hamill Joseph Hansen Chris Hardman Katharine Harer David Harris Carla Harryman Robert Hass Robert Haule Eloise Klein Healy Lyn Hejinian Dale Herd James Herndon Juan Felipe Herrera Jim Heynen Brenda Hillman Jane Hirshfield Garrett Hongo James D. Houston Fanny Howe Andrew Hoyem In. S. Omnia Joyce Jenkins Bud Johns Charles Johnson Alice Jones Joe Kane Karen Karbo Larry Kearney Lawrence Keel Susan Kennedy Stephen Kessler Morgan Kester Kevin Killian Myung Mi Kim Carolyn Kizer Edward Kleinschmidt August Kleinzahler Peter Koch Arnold Kotler John Krich James Krusoe C.H Kwock John L'Heureux Salvatore La Puma Philip Lamantia Daniel J. Langton Jeremy Larner Carolyn Lau Dorianne Laux Larbi Layachi Ursula LeGuin Jacques Leslie Denise Levertov David Levi Strauss Philip Levine Genny Lim Leo Litwak Sarah Liu Barry Lopez Wing Tek Lum Sandy Lydon Nathaniel Mackey Clarence Major Devorah Major Tom Mandel William M. Mandel Morton Marcus Stefanie Marlis Jack Marshall Victor L. Martinez Michael McClure Brian McCormick Ruthanne Lum McCunn Robert McDowell John McNally Sandra McPherson Leonard Michaels Jauren Miller Czeslaw Milosz Janice Miritikani John Mitchell Stephen Mitchell Cherrie Moraga Wright Morris Jess Mowry Melissa Mytinger Nuha Nafal Peter Najarian Leonard Nathan Henry Noyes Tina Nunnally James J. O'Grady John O'Keefe Annegret Ogden Robert Onopa Michael Palmer Walter Pavlich Derek Pell Nicholas Perella Robert Peters Brenda Peterson Kathleen Pheifer Frances Phillips Cecile Pineda Harry Polkinhorn James Pollack Randall Potts Arthur Quinn Leroy V. Quintana Carl Rakosi Orlando Ramirez Stephen Ratcliffe Susan Rawlins Adrienne Rich Russ Riviere M.C. Roberts Kit Robinson Stephen Rodefer Lawrence Rogers Camille Roy Vern Rutsala Kay Ryan Ann Marie Sampson Elba Sánchez Richard Saunders Tad Savinar Leslie Scalapino Donald Schenker Laura Schiff Brenda Din Schildgen R.Schluter Dennis Schmitz P.Schneider Fred Schowalter Hart Schulz Carolyn See John T. Selawsky Tom Sexton Lindsey Shere David Shields John Shirley Aaron Shurin Ron Silliman John Oliver Simon Jack Skelley Edward Smallfield Mark Smallwood Martin Cruz Smith Gary Snyder Daniel Solomon Cathy Song Gilbert Sorrentino Gary Soto Albert Sperisen Marilyn Stablein William Stafford Timothy Steele Lisa M. Steinman John Steppling Frank Stewart Jessica Stone Ron Strickland Cole Swensen Elizabeth Tallent Mary Tall Mountain Kazuaki Tanahashi John Thomas Bart Thurber Sallie Tisdale Stephan Torre Mike Tuggle John van der Zee Nance Van Winckel Victor E. Villaseñor Stephen Vincent Gerald Vizenour William T. Vollman Mary Michael Wagner Alice Walker David Rains Wallace Irma Wallem Christopher Warden Barrett Watten Kathleen Weaver John V. Wilson John Witte Michael Wolfe Terry Wolverton John Woodall Thomas Edwin Woodhouse Dwight Yates Fei Ye Gary Young

LEGEND

Legendary West Coast writers not yet in ZYZZYVA:
Alice Adams Jean M. Auel T.C.Boyle Ray Bradbury Herb Caen Pat Conroy Pete Dexter Diane Di Prima Harriett Doerr William Everson Carol Field William Gibson Herbert Gold William Goldman Beth Gutcheon Oakley Hall Mark Helprin Diane Johnson Ken Kesey Ella Leffland Armistead Maupin Cyra McFadden Terry McMillan Jessica Mitford Jose Montoya Bharati Mukherjee Diana O'Hehir Tillie Olsen Whitney Otto Thomas Pynchon Jonathan Raban John Rechy Tom Robbins Orville Schell Kim Stafford Shelby Steele Danielle Steele Page Stegner Wallace Stegner Amy Tan Joyce Thompson Philip Whalen Sherley Anne Williams August Wilson Shawn Wong

ZYZZYVA
41 Sutter St.,
Suite 1400
San Francisco 94104

Zyzzyva is the last word in *The American Heritage Dictionary of the English Language*. ZYZZYVA is a quarterly journal of West Coast writers & artists. Available at all good bookstores for $9. Subscription: $28/one year.

Subscribe to the leading *readable* literary journal in the US

SAN FRANCISCO REVIEW *of* BOOKS

The bi-monthly *San Francisco Review of Books*, through an eclectic selection of reviews, interviews, essays, and opinions, provides a different map of today's prolific literary landscape, but clearly reflects its origins in the commitment shown to West Coast literature, writers, and publishers.

One year's subscription is a mere $16!

Two years: $31
Three years: $45

Yes, I'd like to subscribe to the *San Francisco Review of Books*, for the sharpest hooks on contemporary books.

Name: _____
Address: _____
City/State/Zip: _____
Phone: _____

❏ $16 (1 yr) ❏ $31 (2 yr) ❏ $45 (3 yr) enclosed*   ❏ Charge my Visa/MC
Acc. No.: _____   Exp. Date: _____

Mail to 555 De Haro Street, #220, San Francisco, CA 94107.
Tel: 415-252-7708   Fax: 415-252-8908

* Check or money order payable to San Francisco Review of Books. in US Dollars.
Overseas subscribers add $1 per copy for postage.

Out on Main Street

by Shani Mootoo

"Mootoo is a skilled writer, balancing uncommon sensitivity and brash humor, able to draw the uninitiated into the worlds within worlds she evokes. Each of the many voices in these stories is haunting and vibrant."

— *Lambda Book Report*

ISBN 0-88974-052-6 $12.95

PRESS GANG PUBLISHERS
#101-225 E 17th Avenue, Vancouver, B.C. Canada V5V 1A6

PALESTINE

"*Palestine* works as a comic because Sacco's a skillful, subtle storyteller, but its urgency comes from the very real voices he's made known." — *The Utne Reader*

Palestine is Sacco's epic, nine-issue journalistic report on the tumultuous history (and current reality) of the Israeli-occupied territories. *Palestine* #1, #2, #3, and #5 are $3 each postpaid. *Palestine* #4 is $3.50 postpaid.

Send all orders to FANTAGRAPHICS BOOKS, 7563 Lake City Way NE, Seattle, WA 98115. Outside U.S. and Canada add 25¢ per comic. Checks and money orders only, please. With VISA or MASTERCARD, call 1–800–657–1100.

The #1 Science Fiction Bestseller!

"Brilliantly realized...Stephenson turns out to be an engaging guide to an onrushing tomorrow."
—*The New York Times Book Review*

"Hip, surreal, distressingly funny...Neal Stephenson is a crafty plotter and a wry writer."
—*Des Moines Register*

"SNOW CRASH is like a Thomas Pynchon novel with the brakes removed."
—*The Washington Post*

SNOW CRASH weaves virtual reality, Sumerian myth, and just about everything in-between with a cool, hip cyber-sensibility. A mind-altering romp through a future America so bizzare, so outrageous...you'll recognize it immediately.

Available in paperback wherever books are sold

Bantam
Bantam Doubleday Dell

SPECTRA

SOME PEOPLE THINK THE BLOOMSBURY REVIEW IS JUST ABOUT BOOKS

IT'S REALLY ABOUT

IDEAS

The Politics and Literature of Central America ▪ Women in Philosophy ▪ The Corporate Culture
The Immigration Time Bomb ▪ Literature and Legends of the American West
Artists and Their Art ▪ The Global Economy ▪ Censorship ▪ Native American Poetry
The Importance of Myth in Our Culture ▪ Controlling Nuclear Weapons.

The BLOOMSBURY REVIEW

A BOOK MAGAZINE

Ask for it at your local bookstore or send $3.50 for a sample copy;
$18 for 8 issues (one year);
$15 each for two or more subscriptions.

The Bloomsbury Review • PO Box 8928 • Denver, CO 80201

LEFT BANK

A NEW WAY TO READ BETWEEN THE LINES — A POTLATCH OF POINTED PROSE, POETRY, AND ART.

New collections in this series are published semiannually in December & June. Left Bank books feature fine writing on universal themes. Readers are treated to a cross-section of creative nonfiction, fiction, essays, interviews, poetry, and art.

WRITING & FISHING THE NORTHWEST — Consider the cast. Wallace Stegner, Greg Bear, Craig Lesley, Sharon Doubiago, Nancy Lord, John Keeble. #1

EXTINCTION — Get it before it's gone. David Suzuki introduces Tess Gallagher, Barry Lopez, David Quammen, Sallie Tisdale, Robert Michael Pyle, John Callahan, Nancy Lord, and others. #2

SEX, FAMILY, TRIBE — Get intimate with Ursula Le Guin, Ken Kesey, William Stafford, Colleen McElroy, Matt Groening, William Kittredge, Charles Johnson, and many more. #3

GOTTA EARN A LIVING — Know the work of two baker's dozen, including Norman Maclean, Kate Braid, Gary Snyder, David Duncan, Teri Zipf, Sherman Alexie, Sibyl James, and Robin Cody. #4

BORDER & BOUNDARIES — Flee with the Bedouins, secede from the Union, travel with Michael Dorris, Diana Abu-Jaber, William Stafford, Sandra Scofield, Larry Colton. #5

KIDS' STUFF — you've got it. #6

HEAD/WATERS — Swim upstream with David James Duncan (The River Y), Marc Reisner (The Cadillac Desert) and many others. #7

BOOKSTORES, SEE COPYRIGHT PAGE FOR ORDERING INFORMATION. INDIVIDUALS, PHOTOCOPY THE ORDER FORM ON THE LAST PAGE, OR PICK UP LEFT BANK AT YOUR FAVORITE BOOKSTORE.

REQUEST OUR CATALOG. AND ASK FOR WRITERS' GUIDELINES — YOU JUST NEVER KNOW.

LEFT BANK

— a great gift to give yourself or any thoughtful friend who enjoys the adventure of superb writing. Just photocopy this page, fill in the form below, and send it today. Or use your Visa or MasterCArd to order toll-free at 800/869-9055. Subscriptions are $16, postage paid, and begin with the next edition to be published. Back-numbers 1–4 are available for $7.95; Numbers 5+ are $9.95 each; add $2.50 shipping for the first book and 75¢ for each additional.

Send Left Bank to me at:

Send a gift subscription to:

I'd like the following editions (see previous page):

My order total is:

I've enclosed a check or Money Order — or charge my VISA or MC; its number and expiration are:

VISA/MC orders (no subs) may now be placed toll-free at 800.858.9055